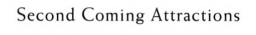

Second Coming Attractions

Second Coming Attractions

David Prill

St. Martin's Press
New York

Design by Bryanna Millis

Edited by Gordon Van Gelder

Visit David Prill's web site at: http://www.sff.net/people/David JP/

Library of Congress Cataloging-in-Publication Data

Prill, David.
Second coming attractions : a novel / by David Prill.—1st. ed.
p.   cm.
ISBN 0-312-18173-6
I. Title.
PS3566.R568S43   1998
813'.54—dc21   97-36515
                                          CIP

First Edition: March 1998

10   9   8   7   6   5   4   3   2   1

Second Coming Attractions

God Is My Coproducer

One

THE GENTLEMAN'S NAME WAS BUDDY FRACAS AND IT WAS APPARENT that he had not been saved.

"Let me explain again," said Leviticus Speck, tapping his business card, which lay amid dried coffee rings and doughnut crumbs on the desk. The card said GOOD SAMARITAN FILMS, with the famous logo depicting the Lord, a number of children, and a flock of lambs, all seated in a meadow before a portable movie screen. Leviticus was not being judgmental regarding Buddy's spiritual status, it was just clear that the man was not a regular churchgoer, otherwise he would have heard of Good Samaritan. "I'm vice president of the most widely respected inspirational film company in the world," Leviticus said. "We make uplifting films, good, wholesome films with a message. I don't need stock footage of explosions or car crashes or helicopter gun battles. I'm looking for beautiful sunrises and sunsets, rainbows, cavorting animals, that kind of thing."

"I've got a clip of a grizzly bear maulin' a guy." He chuckled. "Lemme tell you, it's a *great* shot."

"That's not quite what I had in mind."

"I've got some hurricane footage that you wouldn't *believe.*"

Leviticus spent a moment in thoughtful contemplation. Natural disasters could come in handy, for that wrath-of-God angle. Most of the Good Samaritan library emphasized the positive; even the

Sinners Repent! series was pretty upbeat by contemporary standards, both in terms of the sins themselves and the consequences for those who chose the darker path. Perhaps the most daring entry in this series was *The Bottle or the Lord.* Rance Jericho portrayed an alcoholic insurance salesman whose drinking habits were rending his family apart. Leviticus thought it was Rance's greatest performance, although unfortunately most of his best work ended up in little pieces on the cutting-room floor (most tragically the heebie-jeebies scene). Dad thought Rance's ravings and contortions too intense for his audience, and that the less-than-perfect character wasn't good for Rance's image. In response, Rance threw a chair and took the Lord's name in vain once or twice, but Dad refused to back down. The relationship between them had never been the same, and Rance had since drifted into semiretirement.

Leviticus worried sometimes that they were being too namby-pamby about spiritual battles. In many ways, he thought, we're still locked in the fifties, when Dad founded Good Samaritan. Salvation with a smile, sins washed away with a slap on the back. But the company's still strong and profitable and the films are popular, Leviticus thought, so who am I not to honor him?

"What else do you have in the natural disaster department?" Leviticus asked Buddy.

"Earthquakes, fires, floods. You name it, I got it."

"Any pestilence?"

Buddy achieved a puzzled look.

"Pestilence," Leviticus repeated. "You know, bugs. Clouds of locusts, a march of centipedes, that kind of thing."

"Gotcha." He thumbed through a catalog. "Let's see . . . a praying mantis biting the head off its mate." He looked hopefully at Leviticus.

"Hardly."

"An Army documentary on head lice?"

"Maybe we'll just stick with the natural disasters."

"So that's a hurricane, a flood, a fire, an earthquake . . . anything else for you today?"

"No, that should do it, I guess."

After the order was written up, Leviticus wished Buddy Godspeed and left the sweltering warehouse in Tarzana for the even hotter streets. He always enjoyed his semiannual pilgrimage to Southern California; it offered him the chance to make contacts in the industry, catch up on gossip, and do a little business. But he was glad in his heart when the plane cut through the smog and returned home to Coon Rapids, Minnesota, worldwide headquarters of Good Samaritan Films.

Leviticus' modest affection for the Los Angeles basin was unique among the Good Samaritan family. Dad wouldn't make the trip anymore, although that was due more to an inner-ear problem than any sort of moral objection. This wasn't the case with Evie, who tended to avoid her brother for several days after he returned from South Central Sodom. Leviticus had tried to convince his sister that in order to walk with the saints, you had to drive the clogged freeways with the sinners, but she wasn't buying it.

On the way back to his motel, Leviticus came upon a small mission-style Methodist church, dwarfed by the neighboring In-N-Out Burger and that triune of car repair, Manny, Moe, and Jack.

The modest church sign, lettered in plain white block characters, said:

YOUTH MOVIE NIGHT—THE GOOD NEIGHBOR—
FRIDAY 7 P.M.

One of ours, Leviticus thought with a satisfied smile. *The Good Neighbor* had been released last year. It told the story of Tommie Kare (Ricky Bible), a teenager just like you, who helps out an elderly neighbor, Mrs. Olson (Lovey Molley) by shoveling her walk, mowing her grass, and sitting on the porch with her and sharing his faith. This faith is put to the test when the gang asks Tommie to go to the movies with them, on the same night that he promised Mrs. Olson to stop in and read the scriptures to her. Tommie gives in to temptation. Mrs. Olson has a seizure. If only Tommie had been there. Fortunately, the seizure was a mild one, and Tommie learns his lesson. The film closes with Tommie sitting with Mrs. Olson on her porch, he reading Psalms 13 (Consider and hear me, O Lord my God forth: Lighten my eyes, lest I sleep the sleep of death and so forth), she with the light of God shining on her wizened yet angelic face.

Leviticus wasn't happy with the script when he originally read it. The film seemed to suggest that moviegoing was somehow responsible for Mrs. Olson's troubles. It placed movies in a poor, non-Christian light. It seemed counterproductive. Why couldn't the gang invite Tommie to an amusement park or a rock concert? Leviticus talked to the director and explained the situation. However, Elijah Winds was his usual stubborn, the-power-of-God-is-working-within-me-so-take-a-hike self. He would not compromise his vision, and besides, it was cheap and logistically easy to film someone going to the movies.

Although the vision thing didn't convince Leviticus, a look at the budget for the film did. So Tommie went to the movies.

Even with Elijah's vision, however, the film did not generate as much business as anticipated. This was surprising. They weren't expecting *The Good Neighbor* to be a blockbuster, but it was projected to do reasonably well because of its star, Ricky Bible. Ricky was *very* popular with the young people, especially the girls, what with his curly black hair and dimples, his irresistible combination of boyish mischievousness and genuine God-fearing faith. Unfortunately, the real Ricky Bible possessed too much of the former quality, and too little of the latter. But he was a solid performer, and Leviticus thought he had done some really fine work in *The Good Neighbor*.

So this would be an excellent opportunity to gauge reaction to the film by an audience that wasn't in Good Samaritan's backyard. Leviticus had been pushing his dad for years to do market research, but his elder believed more in praying for guidance than conducting scientific opinion polling.

On Friday night Leviticus headed back to Tarzana and the Home of the Savior Methodist Church. He didn't identify himself to the minister, who gave Leviticus a strong handshake and kind smile at the door.

"I'm from out of town," said Leviticus. "Mind if I sit in on the movie?"

"Please, feel right at home," the portly red-haired pastor told him, spreading his hands apart in a welcoming gesture. Then he said in a low voice, "Don't get your expectations too high. We kind of run things on a shoestring here, I'm afraid. Low-budget movies like this are all we can afford. We're having cookies and lemonade afterward, if that's any comfort."

"Thanks. I may stick around."

Leviticus waited in the lobby, still smarting from the pastor's comments, while groups of tanned young people in blue jeans and T-shirts wandered by, greeting friends and chatting briefly before going downstairs. Leviticus followed them, hoping to pick up a snatch of conversation about the film or Ricky Bible, but all he caught were weekend plans (the beach, sports, a benefit car wash) and the usual Christian tomfoolery. A screen and a few rows of folding chairs had been set up in the front of a large, low-ceilinged room that was used for Sunday school. The teenagers crowded down front, while Leviticus remained standing in the back of the room.

"Have a seat," the pastor said to Leviticus, flipping on the projector. "Jonah, could you get the lights, please."

"I'm okay," said Leviticus, feeling unexpectedly jittery. "Been sitting all day."

The room went dark.

The Good Samaritan logo flashed on the screen.

THE GOOD NEIGHBOR

Ricky Bible

Leviticus had expected a reaction, maybe a spiritually based squeal or two from the female contingent, but they sat silently.

Lovey Molley

Written & Directed by Elijah Winds

Executive Producer Noah Foster Speck

The film opened with a montage of summer scenes: horse-shoes, picnics, parades, followed by a jump cut to the dim interior of an old house. Close-ups of Hummel figurines, family photographs in metal frames, flies trapped in dusty windows. An older woman, white-haired, lonely-faced, sitting on a lace-covered chair. Fade to the same woman outside, futilely trying to maneuver her push mower across her lawn. In the background, a boy is strolling down the sidewalk. He sees the woman, stops, and walks toward her. A face with a set of great, God-given dimples suddenly fills the screen—Ricky Bible, as Tommie Kare.

"Can I help you with that, ma'am?"

Ricky's appearance provoked a response in the audience, but it was not the gushy reaction that Leviticus had anticipated.

They laughed.

Not all of them laughed, but it was more than just the one or two wiseacres that are found in every gathering, Christian or not. It was enough.

The film kept playing, and the laughter kept coming. Not continuous, certainly, but a steady combination of titters, giggles, and hoots. Even the pastor, stationed near the projector, guffawed at times, his body shaking.

What is so funny? Leviticus wondered in a confused panic, his face growing hot. There aren't any jokes in *The Good Neighbor*. A lot of warm moments and important lessons, but no comedy.

Maybe once they get settled in and involved in the story, Leviticus thought, they'll sober up.

"Oh, Tommie, thank you for mowing my lawn. I don't know what I would have done without you. I'm afraid I'm not much good for anything these days."

"Glad to be of help, Mrs. Olson. Did you know that God has a plan for each of us?"

Mrs. Olson's reply was drowned out by the howls.

Leviticus didn't wait around for Mrs. Olson to have her seizure.

On the flight home, the laughter still rattled in Leviticus' mind. Footage of earthquakes and fires were forgotten (he had taken the head lice documentary after all, thinking that if they tacked on a religious-oriented introduction it would be appropriate for Bible camps and youth retreats). It could have been a fluke, of course. On any given night, an audience could react in an infinite number of ways. But why *this* audience, why *this* film? He had no clue.

When Leviticus arrived back in Minnesota, he picked up his car and drove a zigzag pattern through the Gemini Industrial Park, past the small office with attached warehouse that housed Good Samaritan Films, to an old two-story farmhouse set on the edge of the park, a relic from a bygone era.

"You're not going to be able to avoid me for long this time, Evie," Leviticus said to his sister, who gave him a curt wave and hurried down the hallway as he came through the front door.

He found the elder Speck at the kitchen table, hunched over a legal pad, a pot of coffee at his elbow. He was dressed in a black coat and tie, his wavy gray hair combed back neatly.

"Welcome home, son. How was your trip?"

"Fine, Dad," said Leviticus. "I ordered some stock footage. Talked to a couple of distributors. You know, the usual."

"Good, good."

Leviticus hesitated, then said, "We've got to have a meeting, Dad. Right away."

"You're going to have to make it quick," said Noah. "I'm on my way to give a talk to the Presbyterians. Supposed to be on 'Stories of Faith and Inspiration by a Christian Filmmaker,' but they'll probably end up asking me what Ricky Bible is really like."

"Yes," Leviticus said, nodding, "that's what I wanted to talk about."

"Faith and inspiration?"

"No, Ricky Bible."

The elder Speck gave his son a long look, then called for Evie. The trio sat around the kitchen table, and Leviticus outlined the problem. "I just can't figure out what they found so funny," he concluded.

"Let's remember that people are a little different in California," said Noah. "Even the churches are strange out there. We make our films for everyday people."

"They seemed perfectly normal to me," Leviticus said. "You know, they always say trends start in California."

"Well, I wouldn't worry about it," said Noah. "It was just one church. Maybe the kids got into the sacramental grape juice."

"Could be," Leviticus said. "But I was thinking on the way back, What if Ricky Bible is the problem? What if he doesn't connect with the youth anymore?"

"Do you know how many autograph and photo requests we've handled for Ricky this month?" said Evie. "Literally six or seven. He gets more fan mail than Rance Jericho ever did."

"Maybe he isn't believable," Leviticus said. "Kids can see through that sort of thing. I know he's a talented actor, but frankly his lifestyle leaves something to be desired."

"I think he's grown up a lot the past couple of years."

"I agree with that," Dad said. "He's been a good kid."

Leviticus shrugged. "I'm just reporting what I saw. The laughter began as soon as Ricky appeared on the screen and spoke his first word of dialogue."

"We should get better writers, then," Evie said.

Dad looked bemused. "Listen, I think we're blowing things out of proportion here. It was one incident. One. We all agree that Elijah is a first-rate writer and director, right? He's done a lot of quality work for us, hasn't he? We all liked *The Good Neighbor* when it came out, didn't we? Leviticus, I believe you said it was some of his best work ever."

"Yes, but . . ."

"But nothing. You weren't laughing at the film, were you?"

"No, I wasn't, but . . ."

"So who's judgment are you going to trust, yours or some flaky church in L.A.?"

Leviticus was going to say that he wondered if Good Samaritan was making films that didn't ring true with modern audiences, that maybe they should try to update their image. But he didn't say these things. He was afraid. He was afraid that Dad would be hurt and feel less than honored by his only son. And besides, Leviticus wasn't even sure if he believed it himself.

But all that night, and in bed after he said his prayers, he wondered if he was right. He asked God for guidance and direction. He asked to be allowed to see the truth about the laughter *The Good Neighbor* had inspired.

Two

LIFE WAS BUSY IN A BLESSED WAY IN THE DAYS FOLLOWING LEVITICUS' return from California. His column for *Christian Bus Driver* magazine was a week late. No topic even. He called the editor and asked for forgiveness.

"I'm very sorry I'm tardy," Leviticus told Bob Countenance, the publisher and editor in chief. "I just got back from a trip out West. Should be able to send it out to you tomorrow at the latest."

"No problem, Leviticus. I know I can always count on you. How's your dad been?"

"He's great. He sends his love. How are things with you?"

"God's been guiding me down some interesting paths. This month we're doing a special feature on railroad-crossing accidents. Did you know there were three hundred and ninety-seven incidents just last year involving buses and locomotives?"

"That must be something to drive a bus, to have so many lives under your care," said Leviticus. "I could never be a bus driver, that's for sure. You're doing good work, Bob. God's work."

"We're also featuring an interview with a driver by the name of Elroy Huggins, who's operated a bus for an evangelical school in Kansas for thirty years without an accident or a ticket. A very inspiring story."

"Sounds wonderful."

"Oh, there's something else I was going to tell you," Bob said. "I hired a new assistant last week."

"What happened to Rosemary?"

"She went back to the seminary."

"She's a good person."

"Yes, she is. I think her replacement will work out fine, though. His name's Nicholas Puckett. He just graduated from Iowa State. A sharp kid, with a real love for the Word. Doesn't know much about bus driving, but he'll learn."

"You've really been blessed with quality people."

"I certainly have. It's always a tough decision. There were so many qualified candidates. But Nicholas had a strong spiritual sense about him, and he's a fine writer, too."

"Well, I should get going and finish the column. I'll pass all the news on to Dad. He'll probably give you a call."

"Take care, Leviticus, and God bless you."

"God bless you and your work, Bob. Talk to you later."

He had been considering telling Bob that he wanted to retire from column writing, due to his hectic schedule at Good Samaritan, but that wouldn't have been entirely truthful. It was more the paucity of topics. Flipping through a file of his old columns, Leviticus counted three "Who Was the Best Screen Savior?" columns, four entries decrying the moral state of Hollywood, and a pair of fluff pieces on Ricky Bible. Plenty of variations on the same theme. Who Was the Best Screen Judas, Mary, Moses? Rance Jericho, Living Legend. How Do They Shoot Those Crucifixion Scenes?

Leviticus sighed and began tapping at the keyboard in his small office at Good Samaritan Films. He couldn't let Bob down. A friend of the family and so forth. Dad would not be happy: "Such a little magazine and you can't even take ten minutes from your day and write down a few of your thoughts." And he was right. So Leviticus wrote:

THE UNIVERSAL APPEAL OF RICKY BIBLE
There's a lot more than dimples to Christian cinema's brightest star. . . .

A half hour later Leviticus had another column put to bed. He went down the hall to the fax machine, then decided it would look better if he waited until tomorrow to send it on its way.

Poking his head into his dad's office, Leviticus said, "I just talked to Bob Countenance. He sends his greetings."

Noah looked up from the manuscript he had been reading. Removing his glasses and dabbing his eyes with a neatly pressed handkerchief, Noah asked, "How is our dear friend?"

"Very well. Rosemary went back to the seminary."

"How unfortunate. She's a fine girl, a good Christian."

"He likes the fellow he hired to replace her, though."

"Well, that's fine." Noah gestured at his son. "Come in for a minute. There's something I want you to look at."

Leviticus obeyed his father, sitting down at the desk. Posters from previous Good Samaritan productions covered the walls. Over one of his dad's shoulders loomed the Savior, as portrayed by an innocent-faced Rance Jericho in the classic *Hear the Word!* Over the other shoulder hovered the youth-charged visage of Ricky Bible, from *Rebel with a Cause*, his first screen appearance.

"New script," said Noah, pushing a modest stack of pages toward Leviticus, the tears replaced with a fiery, spirit-driven look. "I don't know where Elijah finds the time, but his writing has certainly been blessed lately."

Leviticus gathered up the manuscript, hesitating at the title.

A CARNIVAL FOR TIMMY
by
Elijah Winds

"What's it about?" Leviticus asked, trying to keep an open mind.

"Well," Noah said, warming to the opportunity, "Timmy is a boy living in a neighborhood much like your own. The other boys and girls don't like Timmy very much; he sits in his window all day and watches them play. They think he's mean and crazy and then a neighborhood dog dies mysteriously and everyone thinks Timmy did it. Are you with me so far?"

"I'm with you."

"But then Susie hears her mom talking to Timmy's mom and she finds out that he has a life-threatening disease, so Susie gets the whole gang together and they put on a carnival to raise money for Timmy's medical expenses, and he is the star of the carnival and everyone thinks he's swell and . . . well, I don't want to give away the ending. You'll have to read it for yourself."

"They raise enough money for the operation and have just enough left over for ice cream," Leviticus said flatly.

His dad appeared surprised. "Elijah already spilled the beans, I see."

Nudging the script back across the desk, Leviticus said, "No, I haven't talked to Elijah."

"Have we done this ending before?"

Leviticus didn't say anything.

"What I admire about the story," Noah continued, "is that it works on so many levels. On the one hand, there's a simple tale of Christian compassion. Little Susie realizing she never really took the time to know Timmy, feeling the shame when she discovers his malady, then taking action to improve the situation. That's what this film is, a Christian action film, with compassion instead of explosions, an explosion of compassion, a true parable for our times. It has an opportunity to lift up so many people."

"I can see that," Leviticus said, nodding.

"On another level, it's a universal plea for tolerance, for not casting the first stone."

"I can see that, too."

"Speaking of casting," Noah said, standing up, hefting the script, "I'm going to give Elijah my blessing on this one right now, so he can get a head start on things. Good child actors are always so hard to find, although the Lord loves them all, of course, no matter what the color of their skin."

Leviticus trailed his father down the long hallway to the sound stage. Good Samaritan's latest production, *Eyesore for God*, was in rehearsal, which meant that shooting would get underway later this week. There wasn't much time for refinement at Good Samaritan. Schedules were tight, budgets modest, and rental fees had stagnated in the sixty to eighty-five dollar range. The difference between a film making a profit and losing money depended on small, everyday decisions.

As far as Leviticus could recall, Elijah Winds had never run one of his films over budget, even on the spectaculars. In *The Big Boat*, for instance, Elijah had recreated the story of Noah and The Flood with a water tank, a pair of live sheep borrowed from a nearby farm, and some very creative editing. As with all good art, much was left to the viewer's imagination. Fortunately for Good Samaritan, the era of the Biblical spectacular had ended some years ago, and now they focused primarily on contemporary stories with special effects limited to the occasional dream sequence or angelic visitation. Noah always reminded the Good Samaritan faithful that the more down-to-earth a story was, the stronger the message would be. The only out-of-the-ordinary element in *Eyesore for God*, for instance, was the Voice of God, which is heard by the character played by Ricky Bible.

Fortunately, these days the real God was largely an invisible force. Filming someone praying was the simplest of shots. The effect of God upon people's hearts was unseen as well, except in their deeds. A flash of light at most; better yet, swelling music and a beatific look in the character's eyes.

It was almost, Noah had told Leviticus once, as if God kept a low profile in order to give Good Samaritan a helping hand, a sign that He approved of the cinematic path the company had taken. If God created miracles and wonders right and left, and showed His face all over creation, the only companies that would be able to keep up would be the big Hollywood studios. And the thought of how they might corrupt the Good News was too frightening to even contemplate.

Father and son arrived on the set of *Eyesore for God* during a break in rehearsal. This was the standard Ricky Bible bedroom set, site of many classic moments of reflection and prayer, adorned with baseball pennants, model airplanes, and a hamster cage. Ricky sat on the bed talking to Evie, while Elijah Winds huddled with a lighting technician.

Noah headed over to the director, cradling *A Carnival for Timmy* in his arms like a golden egg in swaddling clothes.

Leviticus sat down on a folding chair at the edge of the set, waiting for the rehearsal to resume, casting an occasional glance at Evie. He hadn't seen her talking to Ricky very often. They were deep in conversation now. He wondered what they were talking about.

Shutting his eyes, Leviticus tried to picture *Eyesore for God* playing in front of the Tarzana Methodists, and what seemed like a moment later, he heard the voice of Ricky Bible, delivering a key monologue.

"What must God think of us, when He looks down from the Heavens and sees His Work littered with pop cans, and candy wrappers, and so forth? We're supposed to be His caretakers on the world. Gosh, if God went to all the trouble to create such a beautiful place for us to live, why can't people just take a second and throw their pop cans and candy wrappers and so forth into a designated trash container?"

Leviticus opened his eyes.

"Good job, Ricky," said Elijah. "You've got the speech down. Now try turning away from the window before you say 'gosh.' I'll lead you into it, just do the turn. 'We're supposed to be His care-takers on the world. . . .' "

Ricky turned.

"Try a faster turn, like you're frustrated and maybe even a little bit disgusted with how people behave. Try picturing in your mind piles of litter in your favorite park. Let's do it again."

Evie had sat down beside Leviticus. Apparently the residue of California had worn off her brother. Usually it took longer.

Leviticus gazed at her. "Did you and Ricky have a nice talk?" he asked, nearly whispering.

She glanced quickly at him, looked away, nodded, then looked at him again.

"What did you talk about?"

"I have . . . concerns," she said cryptically.

"About the film?"

She didn't say anything, then her eyes darted away again. "Yes, about the film."

She had been so defensive at the house about his comments on *The Good Neighbor.* Perhaps she felt too intimidated by Dad to reveal her true feelings about the state of things at Good Samaritan in his presence. Did they share a concern about the direction of the company?

"I have some problems with it, too," he told her.

"Don't you think Ricky is too old to play a teenager?" she said suddenly. "I mean, he's not a kid anymore. Maybe he should be billed as *Rick* Bible."

"Gee, Evie, I don't know," Leviticus said, trying not to sound disappointed. "Aren't most of his fan letters from seven-year-old girls?"

"Maybe we should put him in different types of roles," she said, forging ahead. "Get away from the boy-next-door stuff. Give him a more mature character. He's a man, not a boy."

"Well, he still looks pretty young."

"Especially now that Rance Jericho isn't working much any-more. There's a real void."

"Did Ricky tell you this, Evie?"

She looked at him crossly. "No, of course not. I suggested it to him. You know, I never really took the time to talk to him on a per-sonal level. He's so . . . interesting."

"Have you spoken to Dad about this?"

She shook her head, and looked hopefully at Leviticus. "Would you? He's so old-fashioned. He'd probably think I have some other reason for bringing it up, like I have feelings for Ricky that are other than purely spiritual." She laughed nervously. "Or some ridiculous idea like that."

Leviticus' gaze moved from her to Ricky Bible, and back again. "Well, I guess I can talk to Dad about it," he said. "I doubt if he'll jump on the idea, though. He likes sticking to the formula." Plac-ing a brotherly arm around her shoulder, Leviticus said, "Maybe if we work on him together, we can get something accomplished. You see, Evie, I have concerns about the state of things at Good Samar-itan, too."

Three

THE LINE AT THE DRIVE-THRU WAS LONG, BUT RANCE JERICHO WAS A patient man. Not as patient as he had formerly been, but patient. Once, life stretched before him like the road to Damascus, and everything under God's sun seemed possible. Now, now . . .

A horn bleated.

Rance released the brake, allowing the car to roll closer, closer to the ordering board.

Once, his long chestnut hair hung thickly over his shoulders, and his stomach was flat and lean. And his eyes were deep blue and sharp.

Reaching the board, Rance squinted at the menu. He could make out the oversized photos of the burgers and nuggets and drinks, but the words were a little out of focus. He knew he should probably see an optometrist, in fact had even made an appointment with one at the mall only to cancel at the last minute. Fortunately, he had more than a passing knowledge of what this particular establishment served.

"Welcome to Fat Boy. Can I take your order?"

"Yes, I'll have a Fat Boy Deluxe, large fries, and a chocolate shake. And one of those Fat Boy cookies, too."

There was a pause from the other end of the speaker.

"Hello? Did you get my order?"

"Say, your voice sounds awfully familiar."

Rance's heart quickened. "Does it?" he asked coyly.

"Yeah, you're that Hardware Hal guy! I've seen your commercials. They're great!"

A heart sank. "How much for the food?"

"Four-twelve. Please pull ahead to the second window."

Rance did as instructed, digging through his pockets for the cash. Stopping at the window, he handed over the crumpled bills and change to the worker, a black-haired girl in her teens. She shoved her puffy Fat Boy hat up on her head and gave Rance his food.

"There you go, Hal!" she said cheerily.

"Thanks." He tucked the shake safely into the beverage holder and secured the bag containing the burger and fries in the passenger seat.

"Say the jingle!" she prompted him, holding his cookie just out of reach.

He looked at her. "The what?"

"The jingle. You know," and now she sang brightly, *"If you need some paint don't wait, if you need a nail don't fail, to come on over to Hal's, Hardware Hal."*

What little remained of his patience burned up like a bit of burger at the bottom of a grill.

"GIVE ME MY FUCKING COOKIE!" the man who once was the Lord screamed at the Fat Boy girl.

She got a flustered look on her face, and dropped the cookie between the window and the car. "Ohmigosh, I'm sorry," she said, futilely reaching through the window toward the fallen cookie. She gave up and attempted a smile. "I'll get you another one."

"Forget it," Rance said sullenly, and stomped on the accelerator.

Things didn't improve later in the afternoon when Rance visited the supermarket. A number of years ago a woman stopped Rance in the rutabaga aisle at the Piggly Wiggly and said, Excuse me, sir, but aren't you the famous Christian film star, Rance Jericho? Why yes, I am. I just loved you as the Savior in *Hear the Word!* and *Carpenter Man* and *Judy Sees the Way.* Thank you, thank you so much. Can I have your autograph, Mr. Jericho? You certainly may. And a hug? Why of course. Gosh, wait until I tell the girls I got a hug from the Lord!

Shelved at the time, when Rance was at the height of his popularity, the memory recently had been dusted off, and Rance clung to it as solid proof of his fame. He began going to grocery stores three and four times a week, purchasing only a few items at a time, ensuring another trip soon. Once there, he took a cart and haunted the vegetable sections, furtively catching the eye of his fellow shoppers, hoping for that smile of wonder and recognition, an embrace, anything. But the looks he received were blank or puzzled or friendly in a sort of here-we-are-at-the-grocery-store way. It wasn't what he was looking for.

So in the afternoon following the spat at Fat Boy, Rance returned yet again to his local Piggly Wiggly. Removing a blue plastic cart from the corral in the store's entryway, he pushed it forward, grabbing a box of generic potato chips as he rolled on by the bargain items. He made a loop around the deli and slowed as the stacks of tomatoes and green peppers came into sight.

There was an older woman prodding an eggplant around the bend. Rance slowly, carefully, guided his cart toward her, pretending to inspect the green beans, then as he passed by her, he edged his cart over so that it bumped up against her own. Not a jolt, not enough to offend, just a nudge, to get her attention.

"Oh, I'm sorry," said Rance.

When she did not acknowledge him, he added, "I didn't mean to run into you."

Still nothing.

"Those are some handsome eggplants you've got there."

The woman paused in her eggplant ruminations and looked at

Rance. There was something in her eyes, and Rance chose to interpret it as recognition.

"No, your eyes aren't deceiving you, it's me, Rance Jericho. Yes, *that* Rance Jericho. The King of Christian Cinema, that's how they billed me. I played the Savior in more films than I can count. 'Rance Jericho *is* the Lord.' That's what *Christian Film Review* said. You've got to stay humble, though. I don't have any delusions of godliness or anything, although I think I'm a pretty decent person, which isn't exactly the same thing. Playing the Savior has made me a better human being, I think, and if the audience becomes a better human being after watching one of my films, then I would have to say: Mission accomplished. By the way, do you want an autograph?"

"I am Christian, born again with the blood of the lamb," said the woman. "But I have never heard of *you.*"

"Maybe you didn't hear me. *Rance Jericho.* I've got a pen if you don't."

"I don't want your autograph," she said testily, unsuccessfully attempting to free her cart from where he had her hemmed in. "I just want to get my groceries." Her eyes scanned the nearby aisles. "Help!" she called out. "Help!"

"Fine, never mind then!" he said with equivalent hostility, and wheeled his cart around and down toward the potato bin.

A man in a baseball cap and Bermuda shorts was loitering by the bananas. Rance took up a position on the opposite side of the stack and peered at the man. "Yes, that's right," he said humbly when the banana shopper suddenly looked up. "I am Rance Jericho."

It wasn't a productive afternoon.

Later, Rance returned in obscurity to his bungalow, toting a modest bag of groceries. He checked the answering machine; the red light shone steady. Rance put the food away. Hamburgers again tonight, on the grill. After changing into his baggy white swimming trunks, he stared at himself in the long bedroom mirror.

I still got what it takes to play the Savior, he thought, slapping himself on his white-haired chest. Okay, maybe I'm a little heavier than I was for *Hear the Word!* Big deal. Our Savior probably gained weight during his lifetime, too. He probably got a few gray hairs as well. It wouldn't look natural if I were still a young buck. Maybe I can't play the Boy King anymore, but the Lord of the Last Days isn't so far-fetched, is it?

For a moment, his confidence slipped, and Rance saw himself in a different way. The paunch, the hair thinning and graying and stiff, the wrinkles around his eyes and on his hands. The Savior's hands were important; he healed the afflicted with them, prayed with them, had nails pounded through them. But makeup could do wonders, and hand doubles could be used in close-ups.

Rance shook his head. Why did He have to die so young?

I can be more than the Savior, he thought, raising his arms, flexing his hands. I can be more than the Voice of God, which accounted for his last six roles, bit parts all. I can play any role. I showed them what I could do in *The Bottle or the Lord.* I was ready to branch out, but Noah Speck didn't want any part of it. He wanted to play it safe. Rance Jericho as an alcoholic? May as well show the Savior as an alcoholic. God was working within me then, he thought, inspiring me. It was the right role, and I played it the right way, no matter what anyone says, and the pity is that no one will ever see it, my finest moment in film.

Rance and the King of Kings had traveled through the world hand in hand for many years, but now that Rance had outlived him in a chronological sense, his life had gotten a little lonely.

Rance Jericho *is* the Lord.

Rance Jericho *was* the Lord.

Who is Rance Jericho now?

Rance repaired to the patio and popped open a trio of beers, lining them up on a squatty table beside his lawn chair, baring his body to the sun. Maybe tomorrow somebody would call, and when they did, Rance Jericho would be tanned like an Israelite and ready.

As the sun baked his bare head, and the first beer in line was consumed, new thoughts came to Rance. Why have almost all the characters I've ever portrayed been divine? he wondered. What does that say about me? Am I better, spiritually stronger, faster, than the average man? Am I closer to God than they are? Do I resemble something divine on the outside, or are they seeing something in my soul?

He reached for beer two. It can't be just a superficial quality they're responding to, he mused. There must be something inside of me, something special, something nobody else possesses. That thought made him feel as warm as the sun and the beer combined.

So if Rance Jericho is the Lord, or at least is closer to God than the average moviegoer, can he portray a character that is less than divine? Well, if God could come to earth and walk among common folk, then certainly the actor who played the Savior, this cinema deity, should be able to portray a common man. It may be a stretch, it may take all the acting powers I can muster, Rance thought, but I can do it.

Rance pondered this for a time, while getting a head start on beer three.

The problem, then, is not with me, he decided. I can play the Savior, the Voice of God, the sinner next door, the man in the street, the man in the moon, anything, anything. However, Good Samaritan, specifically Noah Foster Speck, is wearing blinders. To him, Rance Jericho is the Lord and nobody else. Playing God may be enough for some actors, but an artist must grow or he will wither and die like the lilies of the field.

In a short time, Rance felt his stomach pestering him, and he took it as a sign from God, a gentle reminder that he was indeed thoroughly human. As he placed the burgers on the grill, smoke arising, Rance believed in his heart that the world was larger than Good Samaritan and that he had more to offer it than Father, Son, and Holy Spirit.

Four

TELEVISION MAY BE THE OPIATE OF THE MASSES, BUT LEVITICUS BElieved it could be their salvation, too. He tried to focus on the positive and reign in his anxiety as he flew to fabulous Tulsa for another taping of *Quiet Hour Theater*. This popular program appeared every Saturday night on the Resurrection Broadcasting Network, Channel Fifty-six on the Coon Rapids cable system. Every few months *QHT* host and founder Grant Godlee invited Leviticus to help introduce their films and chat about the state of Christian filmmaking during the breaks. They were scheduled to tape two segments this time, for a pair of Good Samaritan releases, *Three Strikes and You're Saved* and *The Bicycle of Redemption*.

"A blessing to see you again," Grant Godlee said in his low-key manner, greeting Leviticus in a cramped cubicle somewhere in the labyrinth at RBN. He wore his traditional yellow crew neck, his face pale but athletic.

"Great to see you again, Grant. How have you been?"

"Very blessed, I would have to say. And yourself?"

"I have to say my life has been pretty blessed as well." Leviticus offered Grant a large cardboard tube he had brought along. "A present for you."

"Thank you so much," said Grant. He opened one end of the tube, then tapped the other side. A rolled-up poster appeared. He carefully nudged it out, then unfurled it. Leviticus helped him display it.

"Nice," Grant said quietly.

The object of his enthusiasm was a promotional poster for *Eyesore for God*. Ricky Bible brooded in the foreground, surrounded by pop cans and old tires and crumpled newspapers. In the upper portion of the poster dark clouds boiled, the sun trying to break through, its rays filtering to the ground, illuminating the litter.

"Came back from the printer just this morning," Leviticus said. He pointed at the lower corner, near a pile of discarded fast-food wrappers. "Look, it's even autographed by Ricky Bible."

"Why, so it is."

"Maybe we could use it on the show," Leviticus suggested.

"A fine poster," said Grant. "Signed and everything."

Leviticus didn't pursue the suggestion there, but made sure the poster was brought along on the long progression through the building to the set.

The set for *Quiet Hour Theater* was a study lined with bookshelves, comfortable leather chairs, and a fireplace: a haven for contemplation and reflection and perhaps some quiet conversation. Blinding stage lights made the set appear more like an interrogation chamber than a library, but the viewers at home would see only the illusion. Grant sat in the big chair, Leviticus took a slightly smaller, shadowed seat nearby. A young man applied makeup to their faces.

"Can you hang around after the show?" Grant asked Leviticus, as the host's nose was patted down. "We need to have a talk."

"Sure," Leviticus said, curious. "What about?"

Before Grant could reply, the director broke in, and soon it was time for another installment of *Quiet Hour Theater*.

"Good evening, and welcome to *Quiet Hour Theater*," Grant Godlee said in a soft voice, smiling modestly. "Tonight we are featuring an inspiring film for you and your family called *Three Strikes and You're Saved.* It tells the story of . . . well, I'll let our special guest explain. He's a frequent visitor to *Quiet Hour Theater* and I'd like to welcome him back tonight. Leviticus Speck, of Good Samaritan Films, it's a blessing to have you on the show again."

"Thank you, Grant. It's a blessing to be here."

"The blessing's all ours. Now, *Three Strikes and You're Saved.* Tell us a little bit about it."

"Glad to," said Leviticus, feeling sweat along his hairline. *"Three Strikes* tells the story of high school baseball player Nathan Deed. In the big game, the umpire rules that he was hit by a pitch, which scores the winning run. However, Nathan is certain that the ball missed him and confesses to the umpire. His team loses the game. How this decision changes his life is at the heart of the film."

"He undergoes some trials and tribulations, then, as a result of his honesty on the ball field," Grant suggested.

"Yes. But this is more than a baseball film. It's about eternal truths and spirituality and the importance of faith and prayer. And I should mention that Ricky Bible plays the lead role. He does a fine job, as always, and I know his multitude of fans will be well pleased."

"Very good, then. Now we invite you folks at home to call the kids, and don't forget about grandma and grandpa, and sit back and enjoy *Three Strikes and You're Saved,* this week's installment of *Quiet Hour Theater.* I'll be back later, when I will have a very special announcement for you. Thank you, and may God bless you."

A moment of stillness passed, then the director quietly called out, "Cut." The camera light winked off.

"Okay, good job," said Grant. "Let's do the lead-in for the other movie next."

"What about the segment for the break?" Leviticus asked.

"Let's get the intros out of the way first."

"You mentioned something about a special announcement."

"We'll talk about it later."

They shot the introduction for the second film, *The Bicycle of Redemption*, a heartwarming story about a suburban delinquent who undergoes a spiritual conversion after stealing a bike from a boy whose family is the poorest in the neighborhood. Everyone at Good Samaritan cried the first time they witnessed it.

Afterward, Grant told Leviticus, "Let's go back to my office and talk."

Leviticus followed the host back through the building. They sat down, Leviticus holding the *Eyesore for God* poster on his lap.

"You know," Grant said, "*Quiet Hour* and Good Samaritan have had a good relationship over the years. Good for us, good for God. I'd even go so far as to say it's been very good."

"I'd go that far, too," Leviticus agreed.

"Good and blessed."

"Yes."

Grant glanced at the poster, then said, "That's what makes this so difficult. I have some bad news, I'm afraid."

Leviticus edged forward, clenching the poster. "Bad news?"

"It's the ratings," said Grant. "They've been dropping for some time. I haven't wanted to say anything, because I was praying things would turn around, but they haven't. Fewer people watching means fewer people are calling in with love gifts. If the trend continues, we'll be off the air by this winter. I have to take action to see that it doesn't happen. You understand that, don't you?"

Leviticus nodded gravely.

"So the plan is, we'll run *Three Strikes and You're Saved* and *The Bicycle of Redemption*, and then, well, that's the end, I'm afraid."

Leviticus prayed for calm and understanding. His mind swirled. There must be a reason for this, he thought. God is trying to tell me something. He blinked rapidly, and said, "Why are the ratings dropping?"

"I don't know for sure," Grant said carefully. "However, in my opinion, Good Samaritan's films aren't connecting with the modern audience anymore. They're out of step with the times. They speak to an America that no longer exists."

A sense of relief rushed through Leviticus. To hear his own thoughts and concerns from the mouth of another, to have numbers in black and white to show Dad, to know the truth. Leviticus lowered his head into his hands, the poster slipping to the floor.

"I'm sorry, Leviticus."

Noah's son raised his head. "What exactly is wrong with the films?"

"It's a feel, an attitude more than anything. The look. The way people talk to each other. Kids these days have to cope with a lot of bad stuff, drugs and gangs and guns and broken homes, so a baseball player getting into trouble for telling the truth to the umpire probably doesn't seem particularly relevant to them."

Leviticus said nothing.

"Don't get me wrong," said Grant. "I have great respect for your father and the work he's done over the years. He's brought the Word to thousands of people. But the time comes when . . ." He didn't finish the sentence. He didn't need to.

"What are you replacing us with?" Leviticus asked.

"Sorry. I can't say. It was part of the contract. You'll have to watch the show."

What seemed to be simple truths within the gates of Resurrection Broadcasting, however, became confounded when Leviticus returned to the friendly confines of Good Samaritan.

"Well, it's not the end of the world," Noah said. "Worse things could happen. It's just one show, after all."

"Yes, but it's so high profile," said Leviticus. "Channel Fifty-six and everything."

"I'm sure it has nothing to do with us. Probably some internal power struggle. I wouldn't worry about it."

"That's not what Grant Godlee said. He told me our films aren't connecting with the audience anymore. They're out of date and no longer relevant to our times."

Noah frowned in a nonjudgmental manner. "How can he say that? Look at *Eyesore for God*. It's an environmentally conscious Christian film. What could be more modern than that? What could be more important than reminding people to treasure this gift which God gave us called Earth?"

"I agree that the message is an important one," said Leviticus. "But the fact remains that we lost an important outlet for our films."

"We're planning to show our films in twenty thousand churches this year, not too shabby if you ask me. Heck, we can start our own show. *Good Samaritan Theater*. I've been thinking about doing it for a number of years, just never got around to it. This will be the push I need, by golly."

Leviticus nodded wearily. "Okay, Dad."

"Say, what is *Quiet Hour* going to replace us with anyway?"

"I don't know," Leviticus said. "Grant said to watch the show and find out."

Three weeks later, Leviticus, Noah, and sister Evie gathered around the television at the Speck house, waiting for the announcement of the new *Quiet Hour Theater*. Evie had popped some corn, but nobody was in a snacking mood. They sat in silence through the first act of *Three Strikes and You're Saved*. When Leviticus glanced over at Evie, who was sprawled out on the big Last Supper rug, she had a look of rapture on her face, and it wasn't the rapture of masses of believers rising heavenward from automobiles and office cubicles and graves, it was something much more earthbound.

During the first solicitation break, Evie rolled to her feet and offered the bowl of popcorn to the elder Speck. "Say, Dad," she said, "don't you think Ricky is getting a little old to be playing a high school kid?"

Noah scooped up a handful of popcorn, "Oh, I don't know. I think he can still pass for a seventeen-year-old. That's one of his strengths. He can play a variety of ages. It broadens his base of fans. He's youthful enough that school kids of all ages can identify with him, but he's mature enough that adults connect with him, too. And senior citizens absolutely *love* him, of course."

"I just don't think he's that believable in the younger roles anymore. I mean, he's almost twenty-five years old. That's an adult in my book. He could be married with kids and everything by now."

"That will never happen," Noah said, nibbling on a kernel. "At least not in the eyes of the public. If he's going to be the next Screen Savior, he can never be seen as having entered into a mortal bond with a female. He must remain pure in image."

"I didn't know you were planning to do that," Evie said quietly.

"I've been thinking about it for some time," said Noah. "I believe it's the next logical step for him. There's no doubt about that in my mind." When the children said nothing, Noah added, "I don't want you kids to think I'm off-kilter or anything. My views toward Ricky Bible are entirely practical. The Savior role is probably the hardest role an actor can be asked to fill, since we are all mortal and born with sin. It's hard to fake perfection; audiences can spot an actor who habitually takes the Lord's name in vain a mile away. So it's an illusion we are trying to create, and even though we know he is just an actor, part of us, however small, must believe that actor is divine."

"That can't be easy on any man," said Evie, hugging her knees.

"It's not easy. It takes a special quality, a special individual." Noah reached into the popcorn bowl. "I think Ricky Bible is that individual."

"Ricky Bible *is* the Lord?" Leviticus offered.

The patriarch nodded, and rose from the couch. "Yes. A new series. I can see it, I can see it. *Bible Stories. Savior Walk with Me.* We'll come up with a name. A new tradition begins. The Bible Era begins. He's going to have to grow his hair out, of course. I'll tell him first thing on Monday."

Leviticus glanced over at Evie, who was rocking, staring at her toes, the look in her eyes alternating between joy and horror.

Before long the midway point of the film arrived. This was the spot where Leviticus should have been waxing spiritual with Grant Godlee. Now, Godlee had the spotlight alone. The Speck family closed ranks around the screen.

"Why, Nathan certainly has got himself into a predicament now, hasn't he?" Grant said softly. "With God's grace, hopefully he'll be able to find his way. With God's grace, Nathan will hit that spiritual home run he so desperately needs."

Grant sipped from a glass of water, then set it down on the table beside the empty chair.

"As I promised you at the beginning of our program," he continued, "I have a very special announcement to make on behalf of *Quiet Hour Theater*. We in the *Quiet Hour* family are always on the lookout for the best in Christian film entertainment. So I am pleased and blessed to announce that we have signed an exclusive deal with Blood of the Lamb Pictures. Beginning next month, we will be exclusively showing movies from the Blood of the Lamb film library. At that time, we will be changing the name of the program to *Blood of the Lamb Theater*."

"Who in God's name is Blood of the Lamb Pictures?" Noah asked for all of them.

"I'm sure there are those of you out there in this blessed land who are not familiar with Blood of the Lamb," Grant said. "Let me assure you that they are a fine, God-fearing, family-oriented company and I know their films will provide many hours of enjoyment and inspiration for you and yours. So circle your calendars for the big premiere show on October seventeenth. Now back to tonight's feature, *Three Strikes and You're Saved*."

The visage of Ricky Bible reappeared on the screen.

"Gosh, Pop, don't look at me that way. I didn't mean to hurt the team. But I couldn't have lived with myself if I pretended the ball hit me. I only tried to do

what I thought the Lord wanted me to do. Can't you see that, Pop? Can't you honestly see that?"

"Has anyone heard of Blood of the Lamb Pictures?" Noah asked again, this time more than rhetorically.

"I've never run across them," said Leviticus.

"Me neither," Evie concurred.

"Well, let's not lose any sleep over it," the patriarch said, scooping up the last remaining popcorn kernels. "There's plenty of room for all of us. A little good-natured Christian competition never hurt anyone now, did it?"

Five

In all his years with Good Samaritan, Rance Jericho had never worked with an agent or signed a contract. All business was conducted with handshakes and verbal covenants. The ways of the real thespian world were unknown to him. He didn't even know where to begin.

Secular film actors live in California, in the vicinity of Hollywood, he determined. That was too big a step, though. Better start slow, small, local. Since there were no motion picture studios in the seven-county flood-control district other than Good Samaritan, he scanned the phone book for a talent agency. There were a handful listed, and he called each of them, getting information without revealing too much about himself. He made an appointment with the agency where he was put on hold for the longest time, figuring they must be the busiest and therefore the most successful agency in town.

Rance slept little the night before the interview. He worried about his age, his clothes, and his hair, especially his hair. It had been long, past his shoulders, throughout most of his adulthood. It was his trademark, his identity. Should I chop it off? he wondered. He feared the fate of Samson. He feared it would make him look even balder. A new image was needed, but he didn't have a clue who the new Rance Jericho might be.

Another problem, of course, was the name. Noah Speck had

bestowed it upon him on his first day at Good Samaritan. Could go back to being Jerry Fudd. Or make up a new name. Rance was okay. Rance could stay. Rance Rogers. Rance Richardson. Or maybe just *Rance.*

In the end, Rance decided if he was going to overhaul his image, it should be done as a piece rather than in increments. Maybe the agency could give him some ideas.

When he arrived at Muttonman Talent Associates, located in a downtown skyscraper with a wheat-field mural at its base, Rance felt confident, dressed in his most fashionable suit—actually a discard from *The Bottle or the Lord,* complete with a small stain on the sleeve where he had spilled some colored water during the heebie-jeebies scene. It hardly showed at all.

"Rance Jericho, to see Mr. Boyland," Rance told the woman behind the desk in the chrome-and-glass reception area.

"Have a seat, please."

Rance did. So far, so good, he thought.

A short time later a young man in a powder-blue suit and shoulder-length curly blond hair appeared from a side door. His hair was nearly as long as the Savior's. Rance immediately experienced a surge of confidence.

"Mr. Jericho?"

He rose, smiling. "Please, *Rance.*" They shook hands.

"I'm Kenny Boyland. Come on in, and we'll talk."

Rance followed the man down a hallway to a small, sparsely furnished office. "I appreciate you taking the time to see me," Rance said, settling into a chair across the desk from the talent agent.

"Always happy to help someone out who's trying to break into the business," Boyland said, opening a green folder and writing something down.

"Actually, I'm not exactly new to the business. I've done thirty-two films. Won a couple awards, too."

The agent perked up. "Thirty-two films? Did you say thirty-two films?"

"More or less," Rance said nonchalantly. "I've done some voice-only work, too, but I don't count those."

Grinning, the man said, "Rance Jericho, huh. I don't recognize your name, although maybe I'm a little too young to remember you. No offense, of course."

"It's quite all right. And you are correct. I did the bulk of my work in the sixties and seventies."

"So you've been in retirement or something?"

"No, I've just gotten more selective about the roles I've been taking. Back when I was younger . . . ," Rance began, then laughed and waved his hand. "You wouldn't believe some of the roles I took. When you're young you don't realize the importance of being selective about your films. Even if the subject matter seems profound, the script is still paramount. Of course, when you're young, you need to make ends meet and so forth."

The man appeared to be fascinated. "Of course." He jotted something down, then said, "You realize that we don't deal with feature-film producers, don't you? We're strictly suppliers for local ad agencies. TV and radio commercials mostly."

Rance hesitated, then said, "Well, yes, I assumed the work was something of that type."

"Not to worry, though. A lot of film actors do commercials. There's no disgrace in it, and it's good money. Keeps your face in the public eye. Who knows where it might lead."

"Yes, that's what I'm interested in doing," said Rance. "I want to be in the public eye. I want to do a variety of roles, all sorts of characters. I want to test my abilities as an actor."

"So give me some names of your films. Maybe I've seen them on cable. Maybe I saw you and didn't know it."

"Well, my first film was *Hear the Word!*"

The man thought for a moment then said, "No, that one doesn't ring a bell."

"*The Man Who Rose Again?*"

"No, afraid not."

"*Judy Sees the Way?*"

"Nope."

"*Judy Sees the Way: Part Two?*"

"Sorry."

"My last starring role was in *The Bottle or the Lord*. I'm sure you heard of it. I played an alcoholic insurance salesman whose drinking is tearing up his family. Believe it or not, some of my best work in that one wound up in the garbage. In fact, that's the main reason I don't work much for that studio anymore. I was typecast with them. I know I can be a versatile actor, Mr. Boyland."

A puzzled look played across the face of the agent. "You were typecast, you say."

"That's correct."

"As what?"

"Our Lord and Savior, Jesus Christ."

"I'm sorry?"

"The Holy Spirit. God Himself. It's all the same, really."

"You've been in thirty-two *Christian* films," Mr. Boyland said, leaning back, no longer writing on his pad.

"I don't care to categorize my work," Rance said. "But yes, you might call them Christian films, although I prefer the term *inspirational*. That's the focus audience, although of course with the arrival of cable the films are witnessed by a much wider and diverse audience these days. The Word is getting out."

The agent took a breath and swiveled aimlessly in his chair. Beyond him, rain began to spatter the window.

"Is there a problem, Mr. Boyland?"

"Tell me about your awards."

Rance nodded, leaning forward. "Sure. Well, I've won the Ark Award for Best Actor twice, and have been nominated seven other times. The nomination is really the same as winning the award."

"And the Ark Awards are presented by who?"

"The Academy of Christian Motion Picture Arts," Rance said.

"It's a handsome award, gold-plated and everything. It's in the shape of an ark. There's a rainbow on it. I can bring one down, if you want to take a look."

"I'll take your word for it," said the agent. "I'm sure it's very attractive."

"So when can I start working?"

"Send us some samples of your work, something we can show to our clients. Your best stuff." The agent smiled. "Your most *inspirational* stuff."

Six

IT SEEMED LIKE A MIRACLE.

The day after Rance Jericho submitted a highlight tape of his work, which had been compiled for the Ark Awards some years earlier, he received a call from Kenny Boyland.

"Mr. Jericho, I may have a job for you."

"Gosh, I didn't expect things to happen so quickly," said Rance.

"Now, I have to be honest with you. There are a couple other actors up for the role. But the client liked what they saw of you, and I think you've got an excellent shot at it."

"What kind of company is it?"

"A basement waterproofing outfit."

Mr. Boyland was vague about the specific role Rance would be auditioning for, but he gave him directions to the ad agency and a person to meet, Una Bonner. After he got off the phone, Rance stalked around the bungalow, pumping his fists, feeling more optimistic than he had for years. He knew in his heart that he had made the right move. This could open up a whole new world for me, he thought. Someone will notice me, someone important, someone who can change my life. I could end up in mainstream films. I could live in Hollywood, and play tennis with other movie stars. I could go to the Oscars, the arm of a beautiful starlet in mine. Chantel, or Brandy. I could make some real money. Or maybe I'd be on a television show. Or have my own show. *The Rance Jericho Show,* starring Rance Jericho. I could go into supermarkets again and be recognized.

Rance celebrated his good fortune with a matching set of beers.

For the audition, Rance wore his lucky suit, the stained little number from the *The Bottle or the Lord* Collection. Finding a crucifix in the breast pocket, he automatically took the chain and moved to place it around his neck, hesitated, then returned it to his pocket.

The audition was held in an office on the twentieth floor of a downtown skyscraper with a soybean mural at its base. Present were Una Bonner, a small, red-haired woman in a turquoise suit, and a man in a black baseball cap and jeans whose name Rance immediately forgot but who was introduced to him as the director. They sat at a long table with legal pads and portfolios and a coffeepot.

Rance was nervous, sitting across from them on a hard metal folding chair, clutching the script on his lap. He hadn't opened it yet. The title page gave no clue:

VERI-DRI WATERPROOFING—Spot 1.

Rance had not been so nervous before a performance since his arrival at Good Samaritan. He remembered getting sick before the first day of filming for *Hear the Word!* It was a heavy responsibility, playing the Lord, but this was a fight to keep burgers on the grill and beer in the fridge.

"You have a very impressive presence, Mr. Jericho," Una told him, smiling professionally.

"Thank you."

"I understand you have quite a lot of experience in film," said the director.

"I've had thirty-two screen appearances," Rance said plainly.

"Very good." The director opened a folder. "Now, Mr. Jericho, I'd like you to do a cold read on the script which you have there. Your lines are highlighted in blue. It's a thirty-second spot, and your part is the lead role."

"Of course." Rance thumbed through the script, noticing almost at once that the highlighted lines were attributed to a character called GOD.

"Any problems, Mr. Jericho?" asked Una.

He shook his head. "No. No problem at all."

Rance got the part, and two days later he returned to the agency, where they fitted him out with the appropriate long white flowing robes and glued a white beard and mustache onto his face.

"Wow, you look fantastic!" Una gushed as she met Rance on his way to the set. "Just like the real thing." She turned him around, fluffing up his wig in back. "Any problem with your lines?"

"No problems."

She walked with him down to the set, which was just a brightly lit blue screen. Apparently the special effects would be added later.

"God, you look great," the director told Rance, as the actor took his place on the mark in front of the screen. "Let's do a quick run-through, and then we'll work on the lighting and makeup. Any time you're ready, Rance."

Rance closed his eyes and took a few deep breaths, centering himself on the Creator. God is mercy, God is love, he thought. God is within me. He contemplated infinity for a second or two, then opened his eyes. Rance felt taller, regal, and a great peaceful power filled him.

"*Acts of God do happen,*" Rance recited in a deep resonant voice. "*I should know. It's nothing personal, just doing my job. But you don't have to be caught off guard. It doesn't take a rainstorm of Biblical proportions to give you*

*a wet basement . . . ruined carpeting . . . damaged furniture . . . what a mess! Don't
let this happen to you! Protect yourself now, by calling Veri-Dri Waterproofing.
Your Veri-Dri Waterproofing professional is fully equipped to give your basement
the care it deserves, the care it needs. Protect your possessions. Protect your in-
vestment. Call Veri-Dri Waterproofing today. Before it's . . . too late."*

"Terrific!" the director said. "What a first take. Too bad the
cameras weren't rolling."

"See?" said Una. "I told you we found the right man for the job.
Congratulations, Rance. You were wonderful."

"Was I reading too fast?" Rance asked, scratching at his cheek
beneath the white hair. "I tend to hurry sometimes."

"Sounded just fine to me. We'll put you on the stopwatch on
the next take."

Always the professional, Rance kept his feelings in check until
he left the agency. As he drove home, he slowly got out of character, and as he did so, his anger began to build. He began pound-
ing the heel of his hand against the steering wheel. His foot
punched the accelerator. I can't believe I went through with it, he
thought. I didn't say a word. I could have walked out. If I had any
courage I would have walked.

Rance didn't see the highway patrol until the lights flashed in
his rearview mirror. Judas Priest, he thought, and pulled his car
onto the shoulder of the freeway.

"In a hurry, sir?" the officer said when he came up to the window.

"Sorry. I wasn't watching. I'm usually a very safe driver, officer."

"I'm sure you are. But acts of God do happen even to the safest
drivers. Each five miles per hour of speed increases your chance of
an accident by twenty percent. Now, can I see your license?"

Rance handed it over.

The officer studied the license. "Everything on here current?"

"Yes, sir," said Rance. "Although sometimes I go by a different
name."

"Is that so? And what name is that?"

"Rance. Rance Jericho." He said it quietly, not looking at the patrolman, not caring if he recognized it or not. Rance Jericho was nothing but a dead end, a God of washed-up actors and wet basements.

"All right, Mr. Fudd. Your record is clean, so I'm going to let you off with a warning. This time. If there's a next time, you can count on it being a different story."

"Thank you, officer."

A different story, yet somehow the same story. A parallel universe where God promotes commerce and people connect with the Creator in the comfort of their living rooms. Where lost sheep with wet basements find comfort knowing that help is just a phone call away. Veri-Dri as the Savior. Getting their feet wet so you don't have to. Walking on the water in your basement. This is obscene, Rance thought. Thoroughly obscene.

The next day Rance got another call from Muttonman Talent Associates.

"Rance, baby, I've got another job for you. Piggly Wiggly supermarket. They're looking for a God type. Manna-from-heaven thing. I told them I had the perfect man."

"When do you want me to be there?" Rance asked meekly.

Seven

ALTHOUGH THE WORLD MAY BE OVERRUN BY THOSE WHO WANT TO play God, convincing a young actor to portray the Prince of Peace turned out to be an ordeal.

"Ricky, come on in," Noah said jovially from his high office, where he was seated with the Good Samaritan brain trust, daughter Evie on his left hand, son Leviticus on his right.

"It's Rick, not Ricky. I'm no kid anymore."

Leviticus looked at Evie, who wore a smile like a proud mother or something more.

"All right. Rick. Have a seat."

"I hope this won't take long," said the actor, tipping up his baseball cap and resting his feet on the desk. "We were in the middle of my big prayer scene. I don't want to get out of character."

"This won't take long," said Noah. "I have a proposition for you. A new direction. A new Ricky Bible. A new *Rick* Bible."

"New, huh."

Noah rocked back in his chair, making his fingers into a steeple, a knowing look on his face. "How does this sound: *Rick Bible* Is *the Lord.*"

"The Lord?"

"Our Savior, specifically," Noah clarified.

"You mean Jesus? You want me to play Jesus Christ?"

"Exactly. We've fallen away from the Savior in recent years. I'm not saying we've been making wicked films, but since Rance Jericho retired, there's been something missing at Good Samaritan."

The elation on the young actor's face was replaced by concern. "Jesus, he was perfect, right?"

"He was the incarnation of Almighty God," Noah reminded him.

"That means I have to be good all the time, then, doesn't it?" Bible shook his head. "That's not for me. I like playing sinners. It's fun. I'd go nuts if I had to be perfect."

"You can't expect him to be perfect," Evie chimed in.

"You're perfect for the role," Noah said with determination. "We'll build an entire series around you as Him. You'll need to grow your hair out, though."

"I like my hair the way it is."

"You'd look great with long hair," Noah said. "Very mature."

"What about my fans? What will happen to them?"

"You're going to be playing the most charismatic figure in history," said the elder Speck. "I don't think you'll have any trouble holding onto your fans."

"Listen, Noah, I don't want to do this." Rick Bible stood up. "I *won't* do it."

Noah gazed at his young star for a moment, then picked up the phone, saying, "All right. You win. We'll get somebody else for the role. Maggie? Could you bring in the file of that fellow who played the mean kid who finds the Lord in *Three Strikes and You're Saved?* Yes, that's the one."

"You don't mean Sephus Jeddidiah," Bible said, sitting down.

Noah glanced at him. "Oh, you're still here? You'd better get back to the set or Elijah will really give your eye something to be sore about."

"Come on, Rick," said Evie, hooking his elbow.

"You can't be serious, Noah," said Rick, unmoving.

"What do you mean?"

Now he was on his feet again. "Sephus isn't in my league as an actor. You can't build a whole series around him. He doesn't have any charisma. You may as well put Leviticus in the role."

"Thanks a lot," Leviticus said.

"I'm afraid that's the best option we have at the moment," Noah said evenly.

"No, it isn't," Rick said. He thumped his chest with his forefinger. "You've got your best option right here."

"Are you saying you'll do it?" Noah asked.

"You've got yourself a Savior."

Eight

RANCE JERICHO'S COMMERCIAL CAREER ENDED WITH SOMETHING LESS
than apocalyptic splendor.

After filming a second Piggly Wiggly spot, Rance went home
and got tanked, and when his mind returned to clarity he vowed
never again to don the robes of the Creator to sell the products of
this land. But when the phone rang one hungry Monday and it
was Kenny Boyland on the line, his resolve weakened. One more
job, he thought, one more job and I'll quit for good. He pictured
himself showing up for the final assignment, being a good God, but
then heaving muskmelons and rutabagas across the store, upending
stands stacked with peaches and plums, throwing the money
changers out of the supermarket and himself out of a job.

"Some bad news, I'm afraid," said Kenny.

"Bad news?"

"Piggly Wiggly has decided to go in a different direction, something more down-to-earth is what I've been told, wisecracking brus-
sels sprouts or something. The clients like your spots okay, but
they just aren't bringing in the customers."

"I see."

"I have to apologize to you, Rance. I thought we were onto
a trend here. That's the way it happens sometimes. I remember a
couple years ago we had a Tiny Tim revival that lasted about a

week. It's unfortunate, but the whims of the marketplace can be pretty mysterious sometimes. I'll give you a call if anything else comes up."

Two weeks later, something else did come up.

"Can you sing?" Kenny Boyland asked Rance.

"Certainly," said Rance. "I'm not Metropolitan Opera material, but I can carry a tune."

"Great. I may have a job for you."

Rance got the job, and he was glad to have it.

It was a hardware store spot and he sang this song, with gusto:

"If you need some paint don't wait, if you need a nail don't fail, to come on over to Hal's, Hardware Hal."

Then the calls stopped entirely. Rance got behind in his mortgage, electric bill, and phone bill. He had to buy his beer by the bottle instead of the case. Everybody wanted his money. For the first time in many years, Rance experienced the sort of muted panic that he'd felt early on in his career, the desperate need for things to happen today, and then nothing happens today. Renewed optimism every morning, hopes dashed by nightfall. Every morning the light dims a little more.

The dim light. It doesn't look quite so dim when you get down on your hands and knees and stick your face close. It looks like a blazing sun. Not dim at all. There's as much hope and as many dreams as ever. But its light does not blind, and the flame can be touched without fear of being burned.

When you feel the cool flame, you know you're too old to start over in some other field, where workers are scrambling after every menial job. Too afraid to pack up and move somewhere else. The only choice you have is to kneel before the flame, and wait for it to dim into darkness.

So when the call came from Good Samaritan, Rance was in an unusually receptive mood.

"Rance, I've got a job for you," said the unmistakably assured solicitor.

"I'm listening, Noah," Rance said, expecting another Voice of God proposal.

"It's consultant work. Easy hours and top pay. What do you say?"

Rance was intrigued but wary. "What sort of consultant work?"

"We're starting production on a new Savior series, with Rick Bible in the lead role. . . ."

Rance's head drooped.

"You see, Rance, Rick needs some guidance, an experienced hand to show him the ropes, give him a few tips. Who else is more qualified than you? I know it won't further your acting career, but I thought if you were looking for . . ."

"You don't need to convince me," Rance broke in. "I need the work. When do I start?"

"Right away, if you're available. Can you be down at the studio tomorrow by nine?"

"I don't want to do it at the studio," said Rance. "Send Bible over to my house. Give me a week with him and I'll have him believing he can walk on water."

"Can you do it in two days? We start shooting on Friday."

"Nothing's changed, has it Noah?"

"We work in mysterious ways, don't we?"

The next morning Rick Bible appeared on the doorstep of Rance's bungalow at ten minutes after nine, wrapped in a loose-fitting white jacket and black T-shirt, baggy white slacks, and deck shoes with no socks. His eyes were hidden behind narrow black sunglasses, his dark hair slicked back. It had grown out some, but still had a long way to go to achieve that A.D. 20 look.

"Morning, Jericho," he said, flashing a smile. "I thought you were retired."

"We've got a great deal of work to do in the next two days," Rance said solemnly. "Let's not waste any time."

"First things first," Rance began, pacing back and forth on the patio in front of Rick Bible, who was sitting slouched down in a green plastic lawn chair. "Playing the Savior is a sacred privilege. Never forget that. Never treat the role as just another acting job. Your heart has to be right. If it isn't it will show up on the screen like you wouldn't believe. Before *Hear the Word!* began filming, I fasted for two weeks. Every day before shooting, I prayed in my dressing room. I took the role home with me. My wife at the time was never treated better in the history of our relationship."

"Why did you guys break up, then?"

Rance stopped pacing. "Religious differences." His shadow fell over Rick. "So, before you begin your acting day, pray, meditate, get your soul in order. Read the Bible. The New Testament. I recommend the Book of Acts. Let the words fill you up. Let His life take you over. Make yourself a vehicle for His power and love. He has real power, the power to affect the minds of men. It's real, it's real. Never forget that it's real."

"Gotcha."

The sweat was pouring down Rance's forehead. It was promising to be a sweltering day. He sidestepped an anthill built between cracks in the yellow-and-green patio bricks and stopped in front of his successor.

"All this happens before you even go before the cameras, all right? Now when the cameras are rolling, what matters is how you carry yourself, the way you speak, the look in your eyes. Don't overanalyze things. Nobody in the audience has ever seen the Savior, so that gives you a little leeway, room for interpretation. If you were doing Harry Truman or some other recent historical figure, you'd be limited by newsreel footage, photos, radio broadcasts, and people's memories. There is a common perception of the Savior, formed by the efforts of artists and film actors such as myself, but there is room there to do your own thing, as the kids say."

"I'm for that," Rick said.

"You should exude love and compassion at all times, because God is love."

"I know how to do that."

Rance did a brief overview of makeup and wardrobe tips, then said, "I know I'm going through all this pretty fast, but we don't have much time. Do you have any questions so far?"

Rick sat up straighter. "Now, the Savior was perfect, right?"

"Right."

"Well, doesn't it get, you know, boring?"

"Not at all. He had powers, understand, and he didn't just sit on his hands. He used his powers."

"Powers," Rick echoed.

"Changing water into wine, for instance."

"Beer would be more exciting."

"I agree, but wine it was, and there's nothing you or I can do about it. Here's another one: the loaves and fishes."

A young face clouded over.

"Surely you remember the loaves and fishes. A big crowd gathers to hear Him speak. There's only a couple of loaves and fish to go around, but somehow everyone gets fed."

"I don't eat fish," Rick said blandly. "Too many bones."

"Could you do it?"

He shrugged.

"How about raising the dead?"

"Now you're talking."

"You know the story of Lazarus?"

"Uhhh . . ."

Rance sat down alongside his protégé. He scrutinized him carefully. "For a Christian film star, your knowledge of the New Testament is pretty slight. Didn't you learn your Bible stories as a youngster?"

Rick shrugged again. "I learned them, but I guess I didn't retain them."

"Well, I would highly recommend that you refresh your memory."

"What for? It's just a job. I learn my lines, hit my spots, go to the bank. Nothing to it."

Rance let the remark go, because he didn't want to pass judgment on the lad, particularly since Rance himself had taken this consulting job for the paycheck. If the kid doesn't want to take the role seriously, then that's his problem and Good Samaritan's problem. Besides, if he bombs as the Savior, that will only make my films look that much better.

But after his student left for the day and Rance got sotted, a still small voice inside him began to speak.

The voice told him that teaching Rick Bible the ways of the Savior was more than a job, more than a means to pay off the phone company. It told him that passing on his knowledge of the Prince of Peace was every bit as sacred a calling as stepping in front of the camera in robe and sandals. It told him that it didn't matter whether he had any stake in Good Samaritan or not. It told him not to say anything about that typecasting business.

So when Rick Bible returned the following day, a morning of dark lolling clouds and wind, Rance was looming tall in the doorway, wearing his long white robe from *Hear the Word!*, and the younger man did quake and gnash his teeth.

Rance took the future Savior to a nearby hillside. Spread out below them was a tapestry of bungalows and parking lots and minimarts.

"If I gave you dominion over all that you see," Rance said, "would you take it?"

Rick gazed thoughtfully at the landscape for a moment, then answered. "Probably not."

"Let's try the robe," Rance said, draping the *Hear the Word!* garb over Rick's shoulders. Funny how different plaid Bermuda shorts and sandals made a person feel compared to a robe and sandals. "Now we'll do a little role-playing. You be the Savior, I'll be Satan."

"Cops and robbers, huh," said Rick, looking pained as he tugged and pulled at the garment.

Rance poked his shoulder. "Look here." Nudging a flat rock with the toe of his sandal, he said, "If you're really the Lord, then turn this stone into bread."

"Food again, huh."

"I don't think you can do it."

"I don't want to do it. I had a big breakfast before I came over."

Rance fought to hold back his temper. "You've been healing the lame all morning and you've worked up an appetite, okay?"

Rick bent down and picked up the stone. "You're bread," he said, sniffing it apathetically.

Grabbing the rock from him, Rance dropped it to the ground and said patiently, "These are temptations. You're not supposed to try to turn the stone into bread, even though you know you could. You don't have to prove anything to the Devil."

Rick thought for a moment, then said, getting into the spirit of things, "No, I won't turn this stone into bread! I don't have to prove anything to you!"

"Good," said Rance. "Now, the beauty of the Savior's personality is that not only does he refuse to do Satan's bidding, he also teaches him a lesson."

A blank look.

"Man shall not live by bread alone . . . ," Rance prompted him.

"Who would want to?" Rick made a face.

". . . but by every . . ."

Rick furrowed his brow, mumbled something, then said, "I don't think I retained this one either."

"But by every word of God."

"Oh, right. I knew that."

Rance moved on. "Now, if you are the Son of God, throw yourself on those rocks down there, because the angels watch over you, and they will catch you and not even allow you to stub your toe."

Glancing up at the clouds, Rick said, "It looks like rain. Maybe we should try this tomorrow."

"And I will ask you the same question tomorrow."

"Well, I'm not going to throw myself down on any rocks. Get that straight. I don't have anything to prove to you."

"I'll tell everyone you were afraid to do it. I'll whisper it in their ears before they go to sleep. They'll know you're a fraud, a mortal man."

"Look, pal, you shouldn't try to tempt me. If I jump off this hill, and I'm not saying I will, but if I do, it will be for my own reasons and in my own time and it won't have anything to do with your ugly face." Rick glared at Satan Rance, and there brewed a righteous fire in those idyllic blue eyes. "What a stupid thing to ask someone to do. Why don't you tempt me to do something that would *help* the world? I'm no damn circus act. Why don't *you* leap off the cliff if you think it's so wonderful, huh?" Rick grabbed Rance's white T-Shirt. "Here, let me help you."

Rance easily broke his grip and lifted Rick off his feet, beaming at him. "You did it, Bible, you did it!"

"Did what?"

Releasing his student and stepping back, Rance said, "Look at you, look at you. You're not the same person you were two minutes ago." He laughed. "You should have seen the look in your eyes! You believed you were the Savior! Not all of you, and just for a second, but part of you, for that instant, believed."

Rick looked at his robe, his hands, the hands that would heal, and pray, and be pierced. Then he gazed at Rance. The kid seemed solemn, a little confused, and definitely changed. "Maybe I did, maybe I did."

"I know you did." Rance placed an arm around the young actor's shoulder and they headed back down the hill. Rance felt a sense of finality. Whatever had remained of his own flame now burned within the eyes, the heart, of Rick Bible.

It was time for Rance Jericho to enter a world without dreams, to drift into retired Christus oblivion.

Nine

THERE WASN'T A PARTY ATMOSPHERE, AND NO POPCORN, WHEN THE
Speck family gathered in the living room on that Saturday night in
October. Leviticus had had to remind his fellow Good Samaritan
executives about the significance of October seventeenth.

"Blood of the Lamb Theater, remember?" Leviticus told Evie and
Noah with some urgency, which was met with obliviousness and
feigned gravity, respectively.

"Well, let's turn it on, then," Noah said, leading the way to the
living room.

"Are you coming, Evie?" Leviticus asked, looking back and
noticing that she was not trooping dutifully behind their father.

"On my way," she said, rooted in place at the kitchen table.

Leviticus tried to be patient with their apathy. He knew Noah
was working long nights, happily plotting the new Savior series
starring Rick Bible. Dad had not truly worked hands-on on a Good
Samaritan film in years—all his executive-producer credit usually
meant was that he poked his head in on the production from time
to time and gave everyone a slap on the back. For the new series
he said he would be a working producer, on the set every day, no
doubt helping Elijah set up shots, offering tips to the actors, rewriting the script on the spot, exercising influence over every stage of
production. The first entry in the series would be a Noah Speck
Film, whether the credits indicated this fact or not.

Evie, on the other hand, was busy but not very happy. Or so it appeared to Leviticus. She seemed reluctant to enter the new era. Even at this early stage, she should have had plenty to do on the promotions side. The Christian media should have been inundated by now with inside scoops on the exciting new direction Good Samaritan was taking, Noah Speck's long and illustrious career, the New and Mature Rick Bible, a look behind the scenes at Christian cinema's most highly respected studio. Something, anything, to build word-of-mouth about the new series.

But Good Samaritan wasn't on the lips of those who spoke in tongues. Leviticus had tried on several occasions to corner his sister and ask her what was wrong, but Evie had been avoiding her brother like he had just returned from sinny California and was full of illicit vibes.

Leviticus himself was wrapped up in his usual troubleshooting duties. For the return of classic Savior cinema, that meant tracking down props (most of the artifacts from the Rance Jericho era were hopelessly rotted or lost), scouting out potential sites for location shooting, digging up public-domain music that could be used in the series' sound track.

But he still had room to worry about *Blood of the Lamb Theater*.

By the time Evie wandered into the living room, the choir of angels was sounding the top of the hour.

The program's logo appeared, elegantly scripted white letters spelling out the show's new name. The logo dissolved into the familiar *Quiet Hour* set, although now a large plaque loomed on the wall, featuring one perfectly healthy, unbloodied lamb. Leviticus thought its expression seemed a bit mean. Heavenly host Grant Godlee sat in his usual spot. Only now he had a cohost. The other man was balding and baby-faced, his lips unnaturally thin. He wore a dark suit and tie. Leviticus didn't recognize him.

"Good evening, and welcome to *Blood of the Lamb Theater*," Godlee said in his famous dulcet tones. "Tonight marks the beginning of a new era for our program. As many of our loyal viewers know, this is the place where you normally gather together with your family each and every week to watch *Quiet Hour Theater.* Tonight, however, we are both pleased and blessed to announce that we have entered into an exclusive covenant with Blood of the Lamb Pictures. For those of you not familiar with Blood of the Lamb, let me assure you that they are a fine, God-fearing, family-oriented company and I'm sure that their films will provide many hours of enjoyment and entertainment for your family."

The other man smiled, his lips narrowing into invisibility.

"At this time," Grant continued, "I have the pleasure of introducing you to the president of Blood of the Lamb Pictures, Paul Pedphill." They shook hands, Grant saying, "Paul, it's both a pleasure and a blessing to have you join us tonight."

"Thank you, Grant, it's a blessing to be here," Pedphill said in a thin voice.

"Why don't you tell the folks at home a little bit about Blood of the Lamb?" Grant prompted his guest.

"Certainly," said Pedphill, turning his attention to the camera. "We at Blood of the Lamb make films by, for, and about families. Our only mission is to support the family, from its very youngest member to its oldest. If we ever fall short of this goal, please let us know." He looked back at Grant.

"What film did you bring for us tonight?" asked the host.

"It's called *The Beating Heart.* It's a love story. I know your audience will be lifted up by its heartwarming and important message."

"I'm sure they will, too," said Grant. "Now as we always say, call the kids and don't forget about grandma and grandpa and sit back and enjoy *The Beating Heart,* the first of what I know will be many enjoyable and rewarding installments of *Blood of the Lamb Theater.*"

The visage of the host gave way to a close-up of the angry lamb. Nothing wrong with the new emblem, Leviticus told himself. There's a lamb in the logo of Good Samaritan, after all. More than one, in fact. A whole flock. Too far away to see exactly what sort of expression they wore. Could be angry, could be sad, could be happy, could be anything at all, when you stop and think about it.

The Beating Heart opened with a domestic scene in an average suburban home, husband and wife going about their household routines. And it was a routine opening sequence, except for the fact that the camera appeared to be anchored at stomach level on the female actor, jerkily moving up to her partner's face when he spoke.

"This is supposed to be superior to our films?" Noah asked in disbelief. "Look at the camera work. Hopelessly amateurish. Grant Godlee must have lost his mind."

"It is bad," Evie said, laughing, the first time in weeks that Leviticus had seen her do anything besides brood.

"I'm not sure what to think of it," Leviticus said, not wanting to pass judgment until he had given the film a fair chance, and even then only if it was absolutely necessary.

Newlywed Jane was pregnant, first time. That much was clear. The camera followed her at waist level to her various trips to the doctor, to the market, to the laundry room. The camera still hadn't levitated enough to allow a glimpse of her face.

Evie exited first, without comment. Noah gave it a little longer, and when it became apparent that a plot was not forthcoming, he joined the exodus, saying he had budgets to work on.

Leviticus held tough.

"Well, Jane and John certainly have a fine family now, don't they?" Grant Godlee said at the break, hands folded on his lap. "And it looks like they will be adding a brand-new member to their family very soon. If you like this film, please call the number on your screen. If you really like this film, please consider supporting the good work you see right here every Saturday night."

Grant spent the next ten minutes soliciting love gifts for the program. Usually that was saved for the end of the show, but since they were trying to launch what was essentially a new program,

Leviticus understood the need to build a solid financial base without delay.

Soon part two of *The Beating Heart* began, and Leviticus fought to keep his attention on the television. Dad and Evie were right, he thought. This is low-budget junk. He felt better about Good Samaritan with each passing frame. His mind drifted and he slid farther down into his chair, as faceless Jane's pregnancy proceeded on course, and the couple chattered endlessly about the child-to-be. Tests revealed that it would be a boy, and they couldn't decide whether to call him Matthew or Luke. They put the finishing touches on the baby room, painted blue with giraffes and tigers stuck to the walls, the crib empty and waiting.

Perhaps twenty minutes into part two, just as the contractions began, the scene abruptly shifted to a shot from a heavenly perspective of Jane and John's house under a dark sky, then a cut to the couple snug in their bed, rain spattering the windowpane. The camera focused on Jane's belly. She wore a white nightshirt, and there was no protuberance. She was flat-bellied. The camera slowly traveled up her clothes, and then her face came into view.

Leviticus sat up.

Jane had a nice, pleasant face. She had long blond hair and a freckle on her nose. She was smiling blissfully, as if enjoying a happy dream.

Then Jane awoke.

She began screaming, then sobbing with abandon.

John woke up. *"It's all right, it's all right,"* he said. *"It was just a bad dream."*

"No," she said. *"It . . . was . . . a . . . good . . . dream . . . we . . . had . . . the baby!"*

John went to the window, his sorrowful face revealed by a lightning flash. He looked back at the bed. *"It was your . . . choice."*

"I know," she said, rocking back and forth, hugging her knees. *"I know."* She shut her eyes and flashed back to that night, the night

of decision. She was spread on a cold stainless-steel table, awaiting the excision. A physician inserted a long needle into her womb, rotating it violently, a malevolent grin on his sweaty red doctor face. Then: buckets of blood, and a jump cut to a mutilated fetus, in extreme close-up. The camera lingered there for minutes, it seemed.

Leviticus felt his stomach heave.

Cut back to the bedroom. Jane on her knees, hands lifted in a desperate plea, as lightning flashed in the window. *"I'm sorry, Matthew or Luke!"* she screamed. *"I'm sorry!"*

THE END

A Blood of the Lamb Production

A male voice, deep and emotional, repeated and repeated and gradually faded as the screen went dark: *"Remember the baby, remember the baby, remember the baby. . . ."*

Ten

"HOW WAS THE MOVIE?" NOAH ASKED AS LEVITICUS STUMBLED numbly into the kitchen, his stomach still rolling.

"Good, fine," Leviticus mumbled, heading for the back door. He walked away from the house, toward the derelict grain bin and the rickety shed they used as a garage. The chill fall air couldn't clear his mind of the horrific images. He stuck his hands into his pockets and paced around the farmyard, searching for answers.

Leviticus tried to distance himself from his emotional response and regard the work analytically. First, make no mistake: Father Speck's quick assessment of the film was correct. *The Beating Heart* *was* a crude, amateurish effort by any standard. The camera work was aim-and-shoot, with little thought given to the overall composition of the scenes. The actors were community-theater castoffs at best, the dialogue they spoke silly and overblown. Bare sets, no music, stock medical footage, butcher-shop editing.

Yet in all its crudity, Leviticus knew that he had never seen anything like it. But that wasn't exactly true. He had seen films like it before, in the secular cinema. The twist ending. Normal life turns out to be a dream, and reality is more horrible than any nightmare. The terror, the gore. *The Beating Heart* belonged on a double bill with *The Last Church on the Left* or something. *The Beating Heart* was a horror film, a Christian horror film.

Of course, Good Samaritan had made a brief foray into the horror genre back in the fifties, when people began to stay at home and let the pioneers of television entertain them. Dad had tried a couple of strategies to break people of their quickly acquired viewing habit, the first involving the purchase of a Coon Rapids landmark. The owner was retiring and moving to Florida, and fortunately he had a religious bent and didn't have to be coaxed in order to offer a good price to an organization that was planning to turn the Lucky Twin Drive-In into the world's first Christian drive-in theater. The Good Samaritan Drive-In. Two screens. Shows begin at dusk. Benediction at dawn.

Every summer night the drive-in shows began and ended with a prayer, piped into each car over the scratchy speakers. At first, the drive-in lot was jammed with believers, who couldn't wait for Friday night to go to the God show. But it soon became apparent that something was missing. Deep, thoughtful films simply didn't play on the gargantuan screens. There was something about the drive-in environment that mandated action, motion, explosions, broad strokes that would keep the attention of an audience who could just turn the key and drive home if they didn't like what was happening on the screen. Yet Good Samaritan's films were typically slow-moving and contemplative. It wasn't a good fit. The crowds became restless and attendance dropped.

Something had to be done, so Noah rushed into production a pair of films that he prayed would fulfill both needs. The first, *I Was a Christian Frankenstein*, brought back the customers, but it was a younger, rowdier breed of believer. The film told the story of a distant relative of the famous doctor who follows his heritage and creates a man out of found body parts. The doctor undergoes a born-again experience and begins the first of what would be numerous attempts to teach the monster about his Savior. He also reminds the creature that God is the Creator, not the doctor himself. The monster seems receptive to the teachings, and the remainder of the film alternates between scenes of the monster going door-to-door witnessing for the Lord and rampaging across the countryside.

The second film in the series was *The Baptism of Dracula.* Here, a Renfield-type becomes a prisoner in Dracula's castle, but instead of attempting to escape or drive a stake into the vampire's heart, he tries to convert him to Christ. "Jesus shed his blood for us so you don't have to shed mine," went one of the more memorable lines. In the end, Dracula moves out of the castle and becomes a Sunday-school teacher.

Noah ultimately decided it was best for Good Samaritan to sell the drive-in to a used-car dealer. The venture had lost money, and the lesson learned was to stay true to one's principles no matter how tempting it might be to ape current trends.

But *I Was a Christian Frankenstein* and *The Baptism of Dracula* were gentle, G-rated horror. In fact, *The Baptism of Dracula* bore the distinction of being the first vampire film in which not a single drop of blood is spilled.

It was a far cry from what Blood of the Lamb was serving up.

On Monday morning, Leviticus made a call to the Resurrection Broadcasting Network, home of *Blood of the Lamb Theater.*

"Grant Godlee, please," said Leviticus.

"Who may I ask is calling?"

"Leviticus Speck."

"One moment, please, Mr. Speck."

Seconds later, the voice of home and hearth and faith came on the line.

"Leviticus, a blessing to hear from you again. How are you? How is your wonderful father and sister?"

"Listen, Grant, I watched *Blood of the Lamb Theater* last night."

"It's good to see you're not holding a grudge. I apologize if you weren't able to call in on the studio line last night. The phones were jammed."

"I suppose they were. All those complaints. I was pretty disturbed by it, too. Almost got sick, actually. If you have to dump Blood of the Lamb, keep us in mind. We're working on a new Savior series starring Rick Bible. He has quite a following among the kids, you know."

"I don't know anything about complaints, Leviticus. There may have been a few. There always are. Mostly it was viewers calling in with contributions. We set a record last night."

When this fact had sunk in, Leviticus said, "I've never heard of Blood of the Lamb before. Neither has my dad. How long have they been around? Where are they based? Who's this Paul Pedphill character?"

"I really don't think I should speak for them, Leviticus. They're in charge now. I can give you the number for their publicity department if you want to talk to them."

"No, that's okay. Let me ask a personal question, then."

"All right."

"I'm concerned about you, Grant. You've run the show for years. You founded it. It's your baby. Are they treating you right? Do you need any help?"

There was a pause, then: "Change isn't easy, of course, but all in all I'd have to say the transition has gone smoothly enough. They're very professional and committed to what they're doing. They don't overlook anything on the business end. Very good benefits, too. I can take off two weekdays a month, paid, and spend time with my daughter."

"What do you think of their films?"

"Now that isn't a very personal question."

"I think it is. You love films."

"Sorry, Leviticus. In light of our former relationship, I don't think it would be appropriate for me to discuss that with you."

"Well, you've got my number. Call me anytime."

"I will do that. I appreciate your concern. Have a blessed day, Leviticus."

"Thank you. You have a blessed day yourself, Grant."

A freak thing. That's all it could be. Happens every time some-thing new comes onto the scene. Gets a lot of attention, and every-one loses their objectivity, but then the novelty wears off, and life returns to normal. Well, let Blood of the Lamb have their day. Hope they enjoy it, too, because it won't last long.

How many films could be made about aborted fetuses?

Eleven

IT WASN'T THE FIRST TIME HE HAD ACCOMPANIED A YOUNGER MALE TO the barbershop, but Rance thought that when his only son left the nest that those days were over. However, Rick Bible had asked his mentor to guide him to the shop of Mr. Solomon, Christian barber, who did the hair styling for most of the stars at Good Samaritan. The ex-Christus couldn't say no.

"Rance, a pleasure to see you again," said the nattily dressed, white-haired barber when they entered the shop, which was located next door to a taxidermist in Blaine. The shop was customer-free. It smelled of hair tonic and musty Bibles.

"Always a delight to see you, Mr. S.," Rance said. "You remember Rick Bible."

"Of course. Noah said you were coming. I haven't had the pleasure of snipping your hair before, although I've certainly entertained daydreams."

"Hi," Rick said.

"Have a seat," the barber told him, using a small whisk broom to sweep off the chair. When the young actor was settled in and draped with a candy-striped and crucifixed apron, he continued, "Now what kind of Christus cut are you looking for today?"

Rick looked over at Rance for help. "Show him your portfolios," Rance suggested to the barber.

"Yes, of course. The Good Book of Looks." The barber re-moved a large binder from a shelf behind him and flipped through it, getting Rick's reaction to each one.

Rance sat down on a bench and picked up a copy of *Christian Barber* magazine, paging through it absently. "Fifteen Reasons Why God Wants His Children to Wear Their Hair Short." "Preperm Prayers." "A Cross in the Window Means $$$ in the Bank." After a few minutes, Mr. Solomon said, "I think we've got a winner here." Rance went over to them. The chosen one was a watercolor of the Savior giving the Sermon on the Mount. His hair was sandy brown, shorter than usual, and somewhat more curly.

"Good choice," said Rance. "You'll look great."

"I hope Noah won't think it's too short," said Rick.

"Well, you can always keep growing it out," Rance said. "But I think it will work really well for you."

"Yes," said Mr. Solomon, "he doesn't have a long face, so the shorter look is definitely the way to go. You'll look marvelous, Mr. Rick. Today I'll just color and style your hair, and then on the first day of shooting I'll fit you with an appliance, which you'll want to wear until your own hair grows out."

"Okay," said Rick.

The barber began cutting. "Nice weather we're having, eh?"

"I wish it was warmer," Rick said.

"Got any exciting plans for the weekend?"

"No, I have to work."

"Any sins you want to confess to?"

This was just Christian-barber humor, of course, trying to put his customer at ease. Soon, not only would Rick Bible feel the role of the Christus, he would also look it, and then, Rance thought, the troubles will begin.

Twelve

CALVARY PROVED ELUSIVE FOR LEVITICUS. HE HAD DRIVEN UP AND down Naugahyde Drive all week, searching for the location where Rance Jericho had first pretended to shed his blood for the audience. Although Leviticus had been just a kid during the filming of *Hear the Word!*, he remembered vividly the dusty, holy hillock wedged between Queen Anne Kiddieland, a low-budget amusement park, and a cornfield. However, even if the Word was eternal, the landscape had changed over the past thirty years. Queen Anne Kiddieland existed in memory and black-and-white photographs only, and the cornfields along Naugahyde Drive had long since been plowed under.

Finally, Leviticus went to the library and searched through the old newspapers on microfilm until he found a small advertisement for the amusement park.

Hey Kids! Meet Casey Jones in person, Saturday, April 9, 12 noon.
Queen Anne Kiddieland, 842 S. Naugahyde Drive.

Going back to the road, Leviticus drove along slowly until he came to the eight hundreds.

Eight forty-two South Naugahyde was now the address for Tire Tyrants, boasting the world's largest selection of tires for your car, van, and recreational vehicle.

Farther east, the cornfield had been usurped by Maniac Video, featuring a two-for-one Tuesday special. It wasn't Tuesday.

Between the stores, the former site of Rance Jericho's cinema crucifixion had been transformed into the Burger Army, a new hamburger chain where adolescents in fatigues marched into battle, liberating a massive stash of the fabled Golden Burgers with magic sauce. Leviticus hadn't been able to avoid the commercials.

When he reported in with the distressing news, Noah responded with a shrug and told him to scout out a new location. His father was religious, but he wasn't superstitious. Leviticus obeyed, and by that afternoon had discovered an undisturbed bluff not far from the studio. He waited in his car as the day faded and the air cooled. At sunset, the light illuminated the hill in a most enchanting fashion. He walked out onto the bluff, trying to picture the sacred events that would soon be depicted there. Yes, yes, it would work. Have to watch out for the power lines there, don't want to get that house down there into a shot. But it was a fine site, nearby yet secluded. Perfect, in a mortal sense. The bad feeling went away. The good feeling, as it always did, returned.

Shooting at the site began later that week. Elijah and Noah both worried that the currently balmy October weather would turn miserable, remembering past Halloween blizzards. So they wanted to get as much of the location shooting in the can as possible.

Leviticus showed up early that first day, expecting to see a petulant Rick Bible stalking around the hill. It was difficult enough to ask an actor to portray the Savior, but to expect him to do the crucifixion scene right off the bat, well, that was simply expecting too much. Leviticus had questioned Noah about the wisdom of this tactic, wondering if it would be better to hold off on the Calvary business until Rick had a chance to walk around in His sandals for a few days. However, his father said that it was Elijah's call, and that he trusted his director.

This trust was well-founded, because it was a different Rick Bible who showed up on the hill that first day. Leviticus watched as Rick, in robe and sandals, his hair falling loosely about his shoulders, walked humbly yet regally onto the set, where the cross he must bear lay waiting for him. The crew members stopped what they were doing and gazed reverently at him as he passed among them, Evie at his side. That was good, he probably needed an older person to help keep his nerves reigned in.

Heading over to his father, who was seated nearby, jotting down notes on the script, Leviticus said, "Boy, look at that. Rance really did a job on him. I wonder how he'll hold up once the camera's on him."

Noah glanced up, squinting at them. "I wish Evie would stop mothering him."

"It's his first day," Leviticus said. "He's probably plenty scared. I know I would be."

Father and son intercepted Rick Bible as he experimentally hefted one end of the balsa-wood cross. His face was entirely peaceful.

"Looks like a good day for shooting," Noah said to his new Savior.

"Yes, it's a wonderful day," Rick replied, gently placing the cross back onto the ground and turning his attention to them. Evie glanced at the cross, then looked at Leviticus.

"How's it going, Evie?" Leviticus asked.

She nodded with some sadness. "All right. This isn't going to be an easy day."

"I know. We were just kids the last time we shot a crucifixion scene. Good times, good times. Remember how Rance used to tease us from his perch? He'd hide a water pistol in his loincloth and shoot us when we weren't looking. We'd wonder why it was raining when the sky was so clear, then he'd start laughing and carrying on."

Evie allowed herself a smile.

". . . sessions with Rance go?" Noah asked.

"Very well," said Rick. "Mr. Jericho is a fine, patient teacher. I learned much about acting, and about life as well."

"That's wonderful, son," Noah said. "Say, I hope our shooting schedule doesn't cause you any problems. I know it won't be easy going up on that holiest of props your first day, but I'm sure you'll do fine. We're all here to help you, Rick."

"Thank you," he said quietly. "The Savior knew early on what his fate would be. And yet he was never bitter about it. Did you know that he once fed hundreds of people on seven loaves of bread and seven fishes?"

"Yes, that's a very famous story," Noah said.

"I wish we could shoot that scene," said Rick. "That must have really been something, even though man cannot live by bread and fish alone."

"That would require a few more extras than we can afford right now," said Noah. "Maybe in the sequel."

Rick Bible may be playing the Savior, Leviticus thought, but who is playing Rick Bible?

Elijah Winds sauntered over, clipboard in one hand, stopwatch in the other. "Anybody seen Griff Grimes?"

He was referring to the longtime Good Samaritan character actor, who was scheduled to portray both Barabbas, the Savior's cross-bound neighbor, and a Roman guard who taunts a thirsty Lord, giving him a rag soaked in vinegar instead of water. Griff had appeared in countless Good Samaritan productions, portraying all types of characters, from a high school principal in *Three Strikes and You're Saved* to a door-to-door encyclopedia salesman on a spiritual search in *Time Out for Temptation*, which gained him his only Ark Award nomination, as best supporting actor. He didn't win.

"Haven't seen . . . ," Noah started to say, then they all spotted the aging, paunchy actor striding across the hill toward them, attired in a Roman soldier outfit.

"No, no, no," Elijah said, walking over to meet him. "You're supposed to be in your thief's costume. You're a malefactor, not a soldier. You're going to carry your cross to the top of the hill and then you're going to be crucified. Then after lunch you'll be the taunting Roman soldier."

"But I'm already in character, you hack no-talent loser."

"You're a malefactor and you're about to be put to a slow death on the cross."

"I'm a malefactor, I'm a malefactor," Grimes kept repeating, retreating from whence he came.

Elijah turned back to his star. "How are you doing today, tiger?"

"I'm ready," Rick Bible said firmly.

"He looks great, doesn't he?" Noah said, clapping the Christus on the back.

"Just be careful not to be too stoic," Elijah told Rick. "Our Savior experienced real pain, both physical and spiritual. Remember when you say the line, 'My God, my God, why hast thou forsaken me?' to think about the words, let them show on your face. He was God, but He was still a man."

"Rance warned me not to act too overwrought, to maintain my dignity."

"Well, nobody said anything about losing your dignity. But Rance comes from the old school of Christus. It's sort of a broad portrayal that could work just as well in a silent film. Audiences have changed since Rance was in his prime. They want a more naturalistic portrayal, someone they can relate to on a personal level."

"Yes, I agree," said Noah. "The same thing has happened with Christianity in general. The Savior has become a personal friend rather than some kind of mighty, far-removed supernatural figure."

"In other words," Leviticus offered, "let a little bit of the old Ricky Bible shine through."

"Exactly," said Elijah.

———

In a short time Griff Grimes returned to the set, in correct costume, and the cast and crew of *Hear the Word Again!* gathered in a ragged circle for the traditional opening-day-of-shooting prayer.

Kneeling at the center of his assembled employees, whose heads were bowed, Noah said, "Dear Lord, bless the production of this motion picture. Let this dramatic portrayal of the Savior's life be true to the spirit of your Word. Inspire the actors to perform in a manner that will bring thousands into your fold. Please, Lord, do not allow the clouds to gather and the rain to fall, for thou knoweth that our shooting schedule is tight. Please keep our crew safe from accident and injury. Please remind us that we are making this motion picture, *Hear the Word Again!*, starring Rick Bible, not for our glory, but for yours. In the Savior's name we pray. Amen."

"Amen."

"Roll 'em."

Thirteen

DURING A BREAK IN SHOOTING THAT FIRST MORNING, WHILE THE crew was down the hill making progress on the coffee urn, Evie stayed on the bluff with Rick Bible, who remained perched on the small platform on the sacred prop, arms crossed, hiding the latex wounds glued to the insides of his palms. He was looking down at her with something approaching adoration.

"I think it's going rather well," he said. "I believe I am really beginning to understand what He suffered through."

He isn't making this easy, Evie thought. It was hard enough trying to talk to him considering their respective positions, her neck was already starting to ache, but there might not be a better chance today. Unable to find a painless way of phrasing her feelings, she suddenly blurted out, "I don't think we should see each other anymore."

It looked like the nails had been driven into his heart.

"Please, Rick, I'm trying not to hurt you, but I didn't know any other way to say it. This is all starting to make me feel very uncomfortable, with you up there and everything. I don't want to date my Savior, even if it's just pretend."

"But, Evie, once I climb down from here and I'm back in my normal clothes and everything, I'll still be the same old Rick."

"It will change you. I know it will. How could it not if you take yourself seriously as an actor? But even if it doesn't, part of me is always going to be thinking that part of you is Him. I don't know how to get around that. I mean, it's not you that has the problem, it's me. I won't know how to act around you, or what to say."

"You always say the right things, Evie."

"And I can't imagine what it would be like to say my prayers around you."

"Oh, it wouldn't be so bad. I could go into the other room until you finished."

"No, you don't understand. He was so pure and holy and everything."

"Listen, Evie, from what I understand, a lot of women loved the Savior. He was everything a girl could want. Kind and compassionate, a good listener, someone who was able to share his feelings . . ."

"But they never knew him *intimately,*" said Evie with exasperation. "There's a big difference. Sure, I could love you like Mary Magdalene, but where would that get me? See, I already have a personal relationship with my Savior. I don't need another one. I couldn't handle it. I think my brain would split in two."

"Rance Jericho had a wife."

"And he couldn't keep her. Did he tell you why they broke up?"

"He said they had religious differences."

"Yeah, he was the Lord, and she wasn't. They should do a book about the wives and lovers of men who played the Savior. I bet they'd find some real sad stories."

"Everyone's different," said Rick. "Rance is a loner at heart. He would have ended up a bachelor no matter if he had been the Christus or a plumber." He flashed a reminiscent smile. "I, on the other hand, am a people person. Just because you play the Lord in the movies doesn't mean you have to live in a monastery." He started to descend from the cross, then thought better of it and just crouched down. "Look, Evie, I'm not naive about this. I'm not saying there won't be problems. I'm sure I'll be pretty preoccupied while shooting is going on. But once the last scene is wrapped up, I'll leave the character with my wardrobe. Won't pick it up again until next time. It seems pretty intense now because I've been in training, and I'm sorry I haven't had much time to see you, but things will settle down soon. I promise they will."

"What about the promotional tours?" Evie asked him. "Your public appearances? Your adoring fans? You can't be out of character for those. The public is very possessive about its stars. They'll want you to be the Lord all the time and the devil with your personal life. You do this long enough, and the role becomes part of you, like it did with Rance."

"No, that's not going to happen to me. I've got it all figured out. I'm just going to do two, maybe three, of these historical Savior films, and then it's on to some serious dramatic roles."

"That's what Rance thought would happen with his career, too. Did he tell you about that?"

"No."

"Then I will. Rance wasn't born to play the Christus. He met Noah at a church picnic. Rance was a construction worker back then, and Good Samaritan was a newborn. He made *Hear the Word!* and it went over so well that Dad cast him in another Savior film. Rance had dreams, too, but the Savior films were paying the bills, and before long the public saw Rance only as the Son of God, and then it was too late for him. He tried to break out in *The Bottle or the Lord*, but his dreams were done."

Rick contemplated this silently.

"The best thing you can hope for is that *Hear the Word Again!* bombs so you can be free of the Christus, if that's what you really want. Of course, if this new line of Savior films isn't a success, then Good Samaritan will have trouble casting you or anyone else in anything."

Rick shook his head, with a disbelieving laugh. "It can't be this complicated, Evie. Our feelings for each other aren't complicated, and that's all that counts, right? We'll find a way to get around these problems. Isn't it at least worth a try? Isn't what we have between us worth at least that much? It's like the parable of the man and his fig tree. . . . "

Evie began crying.

"I'm sorry," he said. "I didn't mean anything." Rick looked into the distance. "Everyone's coming back." He stood up. "Promise me, Evie, that you won't give up on us. Would you at least promise that you'll try?"

She looked up at him and nodded tearfully. "Okay, I promise."

He smiled peacefully and resumed his position. "Thank you, Evie, thank you."

And then they crucified him.

Fourteen

APPARENTLY THERE WERE PLENTY OF FILMS LEFT TO MAKE ABOUT aborted babies, because week after week throughout the fall *Blood of the Lamb Theater* presented more features from their library, each distinctive in their technical crudity, each consistent in theme, each featuring scads of mutilated fetuses.

Doctor of Darkness
Prenatal Massacre
The Saline Solution
Die, Baby, Die!

After the concluding scene of *Die, Baby, Die!*, in which the pregnant leading lady is abducted and hauled off to a doctor's office where she is forced to undergo an abortion, Leviticus went to his father, who was propped up in bed, paging through another script.

"Can I talk to you for a minute?" asked Leviticus, poking his head in.

"Sure." Noah waved. "Have a seat, son."

Pulling up a chair alongside the bed, Leviticus said, "What are you reading?"

"The latest entry in the Savior series. Elijah just dropped it off tonight."

"How does it look?"

"Not bad. Third act needs a little fine-tuning, but it's not bad."

He set the script down. "What have you been up to? Haven't seen you all night."

"Watching television. *Blood of the Lamb Theater.*"

Noah made a face. "Why are you still watching that junk? You're not going to learn anything from them, that's for sure. I'm surprised they haven't been taken off the air."

"I thought the same thing at first, too. But I think they've caught on."

"That's a shame."

Leviticus hesitated, then said, "There's something you don't know about them, Dad. You left before the end of the first one. *The Beating Heart*, remember?"

"It got better after I left?"

"No. It took an unexpected turn, though. See, the mother was dreaming all along. When she finally woke up she had a flashback about her abortion. The camera didn't blink. . . . I've never seen anything so graphic on film. I thought I was going to, well, throw up, to put it bluntly." Leviticus took a breath, then said, "So I've been tuning in to the show every week, and every week it's the same. This week's film was called *Die, Baby, Die!* I didn't get sick, though. I hope to God I'm not getting used to it."

Noah sighed. "You shouldn't watch such programs, son. You'll have nightmares."

"But what are we going to do about it?"

"What do you want me to do about it?"

"I . . . I'm not sure, Dad. There must be something we can do."

"Grant Godlee chose a certain path and he'll have to deal with the consequences. It's not our problem."

"But they're popular."

"Oh, I doubt that. We drew a family audience. What you're describing doesn't exactly sound like family entertainment."

"I didn't think so, either. But I talked to Grant after the premiere, and he said they were swamped with calls."

"Complaints, probably."

"No, contributions."

"It's a fad."

"What if it isn't?"

Noah placed a hand on his son's arm. "Leviticus, the house of Christianity has many rooms. Maybe we don't care to spend a great deal of time in some of those rooms, but we are all family, we are all brethren under the Lord Our God."

"I'm not talking about Christianity, I'm talking about business. Our business. I'm talking about what happens to our business if Blood of the Lamb turns out to be more than this year's model."

"The business is secondary," said Noah. "Our faith must always come first. If we aren't square with the Lord, then the balance sheet doesn't matter. I shouldn't have to tell you this, Leviticus."

Leviticus looked down. "I'm just worried, Dad."

"I'm glad you're concerned. But I think you're blowing things a little out of proportion. Channel Fifty-six isn't the whole world, after all. We must concentrate on putting our own house in order, and with God's help, things will turn out all right in the end. We've got to finish up *Hear the Word Again!* and get Rick out on his publicity tour. Elijah and I have been getting a rough cut ready. We'll probably have an in-house screening by midweek. I'd be interested in what you think." Noah smiled. "Come the Ark Awards, we may have something that the committee will have to reckon with."

Leviticus managed a smile. "You make me feel better."

"That's my job."

Leviticus went to bed feeling somewhat soothed, and his dreams, for now, remained undisturbed.

On Wednesday, the Speck clan, along with Elijah Winds and Rick Bible, gathered in the tiny screening room at Good Samaritan for a first look at *Hear the Word Again!* Evie and Rick were sitting together, Leviticus on the other side of Evie. She seemed anxious.

"I'm sure it'll look fine," Leviticus whispered to his sister.

She nodded, but said nothing.

The lights came down and the film began. *Hear the Word Again!* covered the highlights of the New Testament in a documentary fashion, skipping both the birth and resurrection. While some would say that these were the most pivotal moments of His life, in Noah's view what mattered more was the Word and how it pertained to everyday living. Cheaper to shoot that way, too. The crucifixion scene practically blew the whole budget. So the film was heavy on parables and interaction with beggars, the sick and the lame, and other low-budget folk wandering around Coon Rapids' most sacred vacant lots.

Here was something Leviticus had always wondered about: Did the people living in the Holy Land realize they were living in the Holy Land at the time? If so, did they behave any differently because of that knowledge? Did they visit the various Holy Land sites, like the beach where the Savior walked on water, or the town where he raised Lazarus from the dead? Or were they like lifelong Brainerd residents who had never visited the Paul Bunyan Amusement Center? Maybe this question could be answered in a future Good Samaritan film.

In truth, *Hear the Word Again!* wasn't much more than a standard remake of the original. The story hasn't changed in the past thirty years, Noah had said, so why alter the film?

Afterward, they gathered, minus Rick Bible, in a conference room off the screening room.

"So what did everyone think?" Noah asked. "Leviticus?"

"I have to confess," Leviticus said, "that I had some concerns about the project when I first heard about it. Mainly concerning Rick, and his appropriateness for the role. But I must say he really showed me a side of himself I hadn't seen before. He was sincere, and believable."

"That's due in large part to the work Rance did with him," Noah said. "It was quite a transformation. I wonder what Rance said to him."

"I felt the presence of Rance when we were shooting the scenes," said Elijah in a whispery voice. "It was eerie."

"I do think we need to shore up the middle section, though," Noah said gently. "Those forty days and nights in the desert seemed to drag on forever. Maybe we could change it to a long weekend."

"But it's even shorter than in the original," Elijah observed. "You really need to drag it out in order to get a true sense of what the Savior was going through."

"Yes, that's true," said Noah, "but audiences have changed since then. They like stories to move quickly, especially since we'll be bringing in a lot of Ricky Bible fans." Noah smiled genially at the director. "Don't worry, Elijah, we'll work it out." Noah wrote something down on a pad, then said, "Evie, you've been awfully quiet."

She stayed quiet.

"Was it that bad?" he asked her with a wink.

She pensively looked down at the table. "I don't know," she said. "I guess I didn't think Rick was all that believable as the Lord. He's not convincing at all. He's just Rick to me. I don't like to see him suffer. Maybe we could get somebody else to do the next film. Maybe we could get Rance Jericho to come out of retirement."

"We can't change Saviors in midstream," said Noah. "Rick did a fine job in this film, and I know he will have a long career ahead of him portraying Our Lord and Savior."

Evie stood up. Her face was red and distressed. "But I don't *want* him to be the Lord!" she yelled and ran from the room.

"Well, what on earth got into her?" Noah said. "There's certainly no call for her to react like that. *Somebody* has to be the Savior. It's an honor, a high calling. Why can't she see that?"

"I'll talk to her, Dad," Leviticus said, getting up and following her out the door.

Leviticus spotted his sister as she rounded the corner that led to the soundstage. When he caught up with her she was kneeling on the Garden of Gethsemane set, crying quietly.

Crouching beside her in the felt grass, Leviticus touched her arm. She turned quickly, her face brightening, then got morose again as their eyes met.

"I'm sorry I'm not Rick," Leviticus said. "I think he said he had an appointment at the foot doctor. He's having trouble getting adjusted to his sandals."

"No, I'm glad you're here. I didn't mean to give you a look." As she wiped her tears away, she said, "I suppose Dad is all upset with me now."

"No, just confused. I am, too."

She snuffled, hugging herself.

Leviticus sat down beside her. "Look," he said, "I know you've sort of taken Rick under your wing these past few months. There's nothing wrong with that, and since Rick's mother died when he was just a kid, it's good that he has a mother figure."

Evie made a choking noise. "A *what?*"

"Mother figure?" Leviticus repeated with somewhat less assurance.

"Listen, brother, I may be ten years older than Rick, but that doesn't make me his mother figure. We're . . . we're lovers. There, I said it."

"*Evie . . .*"

"You heard me."

"I wish I hadn't. Evie, what are you thinking? What are you doing?"

"I'm proud of it," she said, rising. "I'm proud to be his lover."

"Do you have to keep saying that?"

"I want to shout it to the world."

"Evie, you can't be serious about this."

"Why not?"

"Because . . . because he's Ricky Bible. The only girls in love with him are under the age of twelve."

"I don't care," she said defiantly. "He's all man, and he's all mine."

"Well, you have to stop it. There's no question. What if Dad found out?"

"Let him find out. He's so intent on grooming people for roles that he forgets they are human beings with real needs. I think he believes in the images he creates. The boyish, virginal do-gooder. Now he wants him to be the boyish virginal Savior. It's not fair to Rick, and it's not fair to me."

"Maybe we shouldn't say anything to Dad. You've kept it secret this long. . . ."

"And no longer. I want to be on his arm the night *Hear the Word Again!* premieres and at the Ark Awards, too. I want people to look in our eyes and know that we're in love."

"No, Evie, no, that won't work. Rance Jericho was married, but you never saw his wife. The general public never knew he was married. We saw to that. It has to be the same with Rick Bible. I can't stop you from seeing him, but nobody must know, Evie, nobody must know." He knelt before her. "For Good Samaritan's sake, Evie. Please?"

"It's a new era," she said with pride, hands on her hips, tears no longer flowing. "Hear the word, brother! Rick Bible and I are an item!"

Fifteen

ALTHOUGH THE INSPIRATIONAL FILM COMMUNITY CELEBRATED Christmas with as much joy and fervor as garden-variety Christians, what they really geared up for was the weekend following sweet Noel, the annual Ark Awards. The site of the awards rotated year by year, and this season the lucky sacred town was Lynchburg, Virginia. Leviticus would have preferred to install the awards permanently in Southern California, but he had no say in the matter. Lynchburg was fine. Lynchburg probably had many underrated, overlooked qualities. Hosting towns had to meet certain criteria, and Lynchburg must have met those criteria, otherwise it wouldn't have been chosen. Lynchburg. Fine.

Leviticus was feeling somewhat better about the state of affairs at Good Samaritan in the days leading up to the Arks. For one thing, America's favorite inspirational film company had copped several award nominations, most significantly Rick Bible for his portrayal of the Christus in *Hear the Word Again!*

Disappointingly, it was the only nomination the film received. Leviticus had spoken to Elijah Winds when the nominations were announced, and he was philosophical about the snubbing, saying the glorious story was far more important than its creators. If the film won just one audience member over to the Lord, then that mattered more than any award. Leviticus admired his bravery, although he suspected the director was hiding hurt feelings.

The film itself was a modest commercial success, but not quite the blockbuster Noah had hoped for. Even a mediocre film about the life of the Savior was guaranteed to draw a certain base audience. So the fact that *Hear the Word Again!* had earned a small profit proved nothing. It hadn't hit that next level. It hadn't created any excitement in the Christian community. It hadn't sparked a revival of the traditional inspirational film. It bore that dreaded label: *respected.*

Concerns about the Blood of the Lamb threat also lessened with the release of the nominations. They only picked up two minor nominations, one for editing, the other for special effects.

Also on the positive side, the apparent affair between Evie and Rick Bible had either cooled or else they were being extremely discreet. Leviticus didn't care which was true, as long they didn't make a public show out of themselves. There were a couple of gossipy Christian movie fanzines that would have loved to get their praying hands on the story.

There was another development which should have been a cause for joy, although Leviticus didn't find out about it until he was sitting next to his father on the plane ride to Lynchburg. After the jet reached a cruising altitude and the peanuts were dispersed, Noah leaned over and said, "You know, they're giving me this award tomorrow."

"Award?" Leviticus asked. "What award?"

"That Nathaniel Berea thing," Noah replied morosely.

"You mean the Nathaniel C. Berea Lifetime Achievement Award?" Leviticus asked in amazement.

"Yeah, that one."

"When did you find out about it? Why didn't you say anything?"

He shrugged. "It's no big deal."

"No big deal? What are you talking about? They only give that award to living legends." It was true. Nathaniel Berea was a pioneer of Christian cinema. He made scores of silent films in the teens and twenties, mostly depicting well-known Bible stories, the most famous being *Last Day of the Son,* which featured a marvelous hand-painted crucifixion sequence. Leviticus grinned. "My dad's a living legend. I'm the son of a living legend."

"I don't want to make a big deal out of it."

"Why not?"

The elder Speck's face scrunched up. "They think I'm a washed-up old man. That's who they give the award to. They should call it the Nathaniel Berea Deathbed Award for Over-the-Hill Film-makers."

"Well, I think it's an outstanding honor. Have you prepared your speech yet?"

"I was thinking something along the lines of 'God bless you and good night.' "

"They might be expecting something a bit more elaborate."

"Yes, I suppose they are. I'll think of it as an opportunity to promote the new Savior series." He scowled. "I'll Nathaniel C. Berea them."

"At least you're thinking positive." Leviticus stood up, hunched over so he wouldn't bump his head. "I'm going to tell Evie."

Noah looked around. "Where's she sitting?"

"In the back. With Rick." Leviticus included the addendum deliberately, wanting to gauge whether or not his father knew the truth about them. His eyes were those of an innocent.

"Make sure they're working on his speech," said Noah. "Have him learn it like any other part. He couldn't ad-lib his way out of a back pew."

Lynchburg was everything Leviticus dreamed it would be. He hadn't been sleeping well lately.

———

A great illuminated white cross stood vigil outside the Dixie Deluxe Inn, located along a fast-food strip on the outer reaches of Lynchburg. While most of the Ark attendees were staying at the Inn, a few chose to sleep elsewhere so they could make a dramatic entrance, complete with stretch limos and high fashion. Noah said he thought these types were acting plain foolish, and Leviticus wholeheartedly agreed. They were camels trying to squeeze through the eye of a needle. The serious and holy subject matter of the films about to be celebrated required modesty in thought and word and deed. Parties were allowed, Good Samaritan was throwing one of their own after the awards, but no alcoholic beverages were to be served and the snacks were to be of a generally healthy, ungarnished nature.

But that was for Saturday night. Saturday morning and afternoon were free. When Leviticus, at breakfast in the hotel coffee shop, complained about the desolate nature of life in Lynchburg, Noah's eyes sprung lights and he suggested that the Good Samaritan contingent take a day trip to Bedford, Virginia, home of Holy Land USA.

"Never heard of it," said Leviticus. "How about you, Evie, have you heard of it?" He was trying to draw her out; she had seemed increasingly withdrawn and edgy the past week. On the plane she had hardly reacted when he told her the news about the Berea Award. Now she was seated beside Rick, who was poking without enthusiasm at a plate of scrambled eggs, and as far as Leviticus could tell, they hadn't exchanged so much as a glance since they sat down.

"Nope," she said.

"That was the original title of *Time Out for Temptation*, wasn't it?" said Elijah Winds, the last member of their quintet.

"Yes, but this has nothing to do with encyclopedia salesmen. I saw a listing for it in a travel book, *Off the Beaten Path of Glory: A Guide to Christian Tourist Attractions.* Or something like that. Anyway, Holy Land USA is on a farm in Bedford. It's not far from here. The guide said it shouldn't be missed—must be a believer to see it. We don't have to be back here until after dinner, and I sure don't want to sit around the hotel all day. Are you folks game?"

They weren't particularly game, but they played along.

So Noah rented a car and the Good Samaritans headed out of Lynchburg on Highway 221, the road to the world-famous Holy Land USA.

It turned out that Holy Land USA was world-famous for good reason. The attraction occupied the entire four-hundred-acre farm of a local farmer. The grounds were huge, so they had to drive through the rutted fields and dales. Every building, tree, boulder, bush, animal, creek, and so forth that could be linked to the Bible had been. Affixed on the hog-house door was a sign that quoted a pair of Bible verses containing the word "swine." A brackish pond became "The Dead Sea." A creek was "The River Jordan." A trio of trees sprouting from the same root was "The Holy Trinity."

Occasionally they came across families and older couples on foot, dutifully trudging from tableau to tableau. These pilgrims looked tired but happy. It wasn't exactly balmy out. Leviticus was grateful to be an armchair pilgrim.

After the rental car had taken a good beating, and much of Bedford's finest Holy Land still lay undiscovered, Noah said, "We should probably head back. We'll have to return someday and really give the place a good going over." He glanced at Elijah, who was sitting alongside him in the front seat, studying the landscape.

"Are you thinking what I'm thinking?" Noah asked him.

The director looked over and nodded. "This would be a very interesting place to shoot a film. But the cost . . ."

"Well, we could fly in for a few days and just shoot footage, documentary-style. Write the story around it."

"Sure," said Elijah, warming to the task. "A farmer's little girl has a serious illness. She can't leave her room, has to stay in bed. But she loves the outdoors, so they move her bed to the window. Of course, she can't go to church or Sunday school, so her father makes little Biblical scenes in the farmyard."

"I like it, I like it," said Noah.

"So father keeps adding on and building and before long it becomes the talk of the county and people from all over the state are coming to visit his Holy Land. Soon they receive enough donations to pay for his daughter's expensive operation."

"Did they have enough left over for ice cream?" Leviticus suggested from the backseat.

Elijah contemplated this for a moment, then replied, "No, not ice cream. A bicycle."

"Terrific," said Noah. "I'll send you back here with a camera crew before we start shooting Rick's next picture."

"Can I play the farmer?" Rick asked hopefully, sitting in the back between Evie and the window.

"No, you're going to be too busy with the Savior series," Noah said.

"I think I'd be perfect for the part," said Rick. "I can play a farmer."

"Have you ever played a farmer before?" Noah asked him a shade patronizingly.

"Well, no. But I don't think it would be any more difficult than playing the Son of God."

"You need to have technical expertise to play a farmer, some knowledge about modern-day agribusiness," said Noah. "Which came first, the chicken or the egg?"

"I . . . I'm not sure."

"Don't worry, we'll find somebody else."

Rick's lips tightened and he stared out the window. Evie sank an inch lower in her seat, gazing straight ahead.

Before they bid adieu to Holy Land USA, the Good Samaritan gang visited the gift shop. Noah bought Rick a six-dollar crown of thorns and a half-dozen cut nails (three for a buck), the attached card stating that they were "similar to the nails used to crucify our Lord."

Sixteen

Movies, movies, Christian movies
Praise the Lord and pass the popcorn
It's a swell night to be reborn
Matthew, Mark, Luke, and John
They're all here tonight
They'll all find out who will win tonight
Tonight, tonight, Christian movies
All the sinners will be winners
Tonight!

THE CHOIR OF HEAVENLY HOSTS WHICH OPENED THE ARK AWARDS ceremony wobbled as they floated offstage, reeled in by a stagehand not quite out of sight behind the curtains. The audience applauded modestly. Some didn't clap at all, apparently thinking they were in church. Leviticus never understood why this custom of not acknowledging performers had persisted in certain Christian churches. Was there some Biblical reference regarding the matter he had overlooked? Perhaps applause was seen as a form of worship, and in God's house, there was only one performer who should get any ovations (actually it was a three-ring act, but they all received equal billing).

Leviticus understood. He had grown up around the church and

had learned to tolerate its idiosyncrasies. He briefly clapped for the angels, then, feeling self-conscious, returned his hands to his lap.

After a few more semientertaining preliminaries, the highlight being a dog act involving a hoop and a burning bush, the award presentations commenced.

The emcee, V. D. "Buck" Verily, longtime publisher of *Christian Film Review*, opened the meat of the ceremony with a prayer. And then there wasn't light. Finally, a spotlight found the podium.

"Dear Lord, bless our award ceremony. We pray that Your wisdom guided the hand of the judges in making their very difficult decisions. We praise all the nominees. The last shall be first, and the first shall be last, because yea, the nomination is the award. May all the works praised tonight lift up the lives of Your people, and may this night inspire others to create works which glorify Your name. Amen."

"Amen."

"May I have the envelope, please."

Buck Verily was getting a little ahead of himself, but before long the first winners were announced in several minor categories. Leviticus was keeping tabs on *Blood of the Lamb*. They lost the awards for editing and special effects. That was unfortunate. Leviticus was hoping they would win so he could get a gander at their table and see what an angry lamb looked like.

Good Samaritan's luck wasn't any better in the minor categories, losing out in the best costume and best original prayer categories. After the latter award had been announced, there was a brief entertainment interlude featuring Christian magician Doug Hosannah. Leviticus had witnessed his act at a convention in Los Angeles a couple years ago. He was a reasonably talented fellow whose innocuous feats of legerdemain highlighted inspirational episodes from the life of the Lord. Magic was generally frowned upon in the Christian community as a tool of Satan, but this wasn't real magic, it was the world of illusion, and since illusion was based on human perception, and God created humans, then illusory magic was a perfectly acceptable activity, made even better if it glorified His name.

Doug Hosannah opened with some sleight of hand. Placing a red watch with large numbers into his left palm, he closed both hands, holding his arms straight out, fists pointing at the audience. He stepped to the edge of the low stage, the table adjacent to the Good Samaritan camp. "Which hand is the watch in?" he asked a woman in a green gown.

She laughed self-consciously, face reddening, then patted the knuckles of his left hand. Good choice, Leviticus thought. He had seen the magician slip the watch into his left palm. The hand closed around it and had not opened since.

Hosannah slowly unfolded his left hand.

No watch there.

She tapped his right fist.

Or there.

The magician looked befuddled, searching his suit and pants pockets, then stood there confused with his hands on his hips. After an exaggerated shrug, he reached toward the woman, a smile growing on his face. He took her left hand, which was closed at the moment, turned it over, and uncurled her fingers.

He had found the watch.

Taking the timepiece from the startled woman, he held it up before the audience. At first it appeared to be the same watch, but now Leviticus noticed that it was different in one important respect.

The watch had no hands or numbers.

"As the Lord our God has told us," the magician said in a deep voice, "you will not know the day nor the hour when the Son of God will return to reclaim his rightful place as the King of Kings. He will come like a thief in the night. Be prepared. Always be prepared."

After a balancing trick involving a glass of sacramental wine and a spoon, which apparently demonstrated God's eternal forgiveness in a manner which Leviticus did not quite fathom, Doug Hosannah brought out that most hoary of illusionist apparatus, the black top hat.

"Now, my friends in the Lord," said Hosannah, "have you ever seen someone pull a lamb out of a hat?"

The magician's hand dove deep into the big hat.

What he removed was not a lamb.

As he had placed his hand into the top hat, he was already giving the audience his jaunty magician look. But then the jauntiness changed to confusion, and then to shock as he extracted the bloody thing that resided in the hat.

Some in the audience gasped.

Not a lamb, but a mutilated fetus, dripping blood. Hosannah quickly returned the fetus to its point of origin. He frantically dug around in the hat, appeared to latch onto something, then yanked it out.

A squirming, nonaborted baby, wrapped in a swaddling blue T-shirt. Smiling in relief, the magician held up the child for the audience, which clapped with equal relief.

Now an inscription on the T-shirt could be seen:

Thanks, Mom, for Choosing Life

Hosannah had more paraphernalia in place on the stage, but apparently figured this was a trick that couldn't be topped, so while the applause still rang heartily he ran offstage, pressing the infant to his bosom.

The old fetus-in-the-top-hat trick, Leviticus thought darkly. That baby had Blood of the Lamb written all over him. This will steal the show, and the headlines later on. The Nathaniel C. Berea Award will be a footnote in the accounts of the evening. So even though Blood of the Lamb got shut out in the awards department, they won the publicity battle. This development was disturbing, coming after the hijacking of *Quiet Hour Theater.* Even though they were inept filmmakers, their self-promotional tactics appeared to be boundless.

However, a factor that boded well for Good Samaritan, Leviticus figured, was that shock tactics such as those displayed this evening had a very short shelf life. At some point Blood of the Lamb would have to deliver the goods. They would have to make a film that rose above their previous abysmal efforts. Nothing Leviticus had seen even remotely indicated that they were prepared to do this. Their time would be past soon, and next year all lambs would be meek again.

The ceremony seemed to lag after the fetal trick, although there were glad tidings of great joy at the Good Samaritan table, with the exception of Leviticus' sister, when Rick Bible won the best actor award for his portrayal of the Christus in *Hear the Word Again!* Rick himself didn't appear to be particularly thrilled, but he made the short trip to the stage anyway, putting on his best Ricky Bible smile before he accepted the Ark and stepped to the microphone.

"Thank you very much for this award," he began. "It's the most, uh, exciting night of my life. It was an honor to portray our Savior, and I hope to do it, I hope to . . . well, gosh, I'd just like to thank all the kind folks at Good Samaritan Films, without whom this movie would never have been made. Thank you all, thank you very much." Rick hurried off the stage.

Panic swept across the Good Samaritan table as Rick sat down, setting his Ark on the table. Noah held his head in his hands. Elijah had shut his eyes. Even Evie looked dismayed. Leviticus hadn't caught on at first, but then it struck him as it had hit the other Good Samaritans moments before.

Rick Bible had not thanked God.

It was the ultimate faux pas at the Arks. Leviticus could not recall another instance when a winner had not thanked God at least once. Two or three times was considered normal, four or five a bit overdoing it, one the absolute minimum. But to not thank God even once was unprecedented.

Evie leaned close to Rick and whispered urgently in his ear. His face blanched, and he started out of his chair for the stage, but then saw that he was too late. Buck Verily had already begun introducing the nominees for best picture. Rick disconsolately sat back down.

The Ark Award for best picture went to a documentary called *Heart of Lightness,* which told the story of a group of missionaries and their work in New Guinea. Leviticus had not seen it. The clip they had shown looked pretty good, though. It had beaten out *Crusader Preacher,* a fictional portrayal of the life of Billy Graham and *The Sun-Clothed Woman,* an animated puppet show about the Book of Revelations.

The crowd grew noticeably restless after the best picture Ark, but there was still one very important award remaining, as Buck Verily informed them.

"Tonight it is my high honor and privilege," he began, "to present the annual Nathaniel C. Berea Lifetime Achievement Award, which is given to the individual who is judged to have done the most to advance the cause of Christian filmmaking throughout the course of a lifetime. The award is named after Nathaniel Berea, who invented the inspirational film. This year's winner is no stranger to you in this room tonight. For over forty years he has been the head of what is widely considered to be the most respected studio in the industry. His films have been enjoyed by thousands of families across the world. His list of films reads like a litany of classic Christian film entertainment. *Hear the Word! Time Out for Temptation. Judy Sees the Way.*"

There was a smattering of applause.

"Ladies and gentlemen, friends in the Lord, it is my great pleasure and distinct honor to introduce to you the winner of this year's Nathaniel C. Berea Award, Noah Foster Speck."

More reasonably heartfelt applause accompanied Father Speck as he slowly rose, his expression gracious and wise, and stepped up to the podium. After accepting the award from V. D. Verily—and it was a beaut: a gold-plated replica of the Ten Commandments tablets with the names of past winners inscribed where the sins should be—Noah leaned in toward the microphone.

"Well, this is really something. I'm not sure how to express my gratitude at being presented with such a wonderful honor. I've been blessed with a fine family, my daughter Evie and son Leviticus, and of course the late Mrs. Speck, may she rest in peace. And all the wonderful people who work at Good Samaritan, every last one of them is so important, and I appreciate the work they do more than I've ever been able to tell them. So I'd like to accept this award on behalf of them as well."

Noah looked down at his family. Leviticus smiled at his father, eyes blurry with tears.

"If there is a legacy I would like to leave with Good Samaritan—and listen, I can tell you right now it will be a long time before I'm ready to leave anything—then that would be what Buck said about me in his introduction. Good Samaritan's films have been enjoyed by thousands of families across the world. Think about that for a minute. Enjoyment. We make Christian films, films with a message, The Message, but we never forget that we aren't delivering the Word—the Bible is the only source for that—we're trying to give people entertainment. We have modest goals. Love your neighbor as God loves you. Develop a personal relationship with your Savior. Be a Good Samaritan. To me, these are things that define the traditional Christian film. They're inspirational films. Nothing too complicated. But I don't sit around trying to define things." He laughed. "I'm too busy making movies. And I hope to make many more before I go join Nathaniel Berea in the higher kingdom. Thank you all so much, and thanks be to God for giving me the filmmaker's gift. God bless you all."

Noah was swept back into his seat with a hearty ovation by middle-class Christian standards.

Retaking his place at the podium, Buck Verily said, "It's been a wonderful, blessed night." Organ music, some unidentifiable but familiar hymn, wafted through the hall. "Before we say the closing prayer, I would ask that any of you in the audience who were touched by the film clips you saw here tonight and are ready to accept the Lord Jesus Christ as your personal Savior, to please come forward at this time. You may have never committed your life to the Lord, you may have had a close relationship with the Lord in the past but have fallen away in recent years, you may want to renew your faith for whatever reason. Please come to the front of the room now."

A few souls left their tables and took the walk.

"When you get up here a counselor will talk with you and give you information to help you on your pathway back to the Lord."

Leviticus surveyed the Good Samaritan table. Nobody seemed inclined to join the procession. Why should they? he thought, what with the new award-winning Christus and this year's recipient of the Nathaniel Berea Award.

"Yes, yes, come forward," Buck said, nodding. "Praise the Lord and pass the popcorn. It's a *swell* night to be reborn."

Seventeen

It looked as though seven loaves and three fishes would be more than enough to feed the missing multitudes at Good Samaritan's after-Ark party. They had rented a pair of suites for the event. In past years the party was respectably well-attended, and this year expectations were higher because of the newly crowned Christus and the Nathaniel Berea honoree.

The spread wasn't plentiful, more Last Supper than last meal. Cheese and crackers. Grapes. Peanuts. Punch. Angel food cake.

Noah and Elijah were seated on a sofa, engaged in a soft, animated conversation. Rick, looking morose, was pouring himself a glass of punch. Evie was nowhere to be seen.

"Cheer up, Rick," said Leviticus, popping a grape into his mouth. "It wasn't the worst mistake ever. You could even make the case that it's inappropriate for someone who won an award for portraying the Savior to thank God in his acceptance speech. Who knows, you might even start a trend; maybe next year not thanking God will be de rigueur for the modest Christian actor."

Rick chugged down a glass of punch without acknowledging Leviticus.

"Don't let it spoil your evening," Leviticus told him. "You'll look back on this as one of the great moments of your life. You don't want to remember this as a sad occasion, do you?"

The new Christus looked at Leviticus as if he had not heard a word of his pep talk. "Have you seen Evie?"

"No, I haven't seen her since the awards broke up. She probably just ran into someone she knew. Not to worry, big guy."

Leviticus wandered over to the sofa, picking up the Berea Award from its place on the end table. Heavy. Dad's name was about in the spot where "Thou shalt not covet thy neighbor's wife" would have been. He was careful not to let it slip from his hands.

"What's bothering the boy?" Noah asked Leviticus in a low voice.

"Oh, I think he's just upset about the thanking-God thing. I told him not to let it ruin his evening."

"Good."

"He's a sensitive soul," observed Elijah, sweeping cracker crumbs off his black dress slacks.

Setting the statue back down, Leviticus said, "I was expecting a little better turn out. I wonder where everyone is?"

Motioning to the door, Noah said, "Here they come."

Actually, it was a singular partygoer. V. D. Verily, tie loosened and a finger hooked onto the collar of his burgundy emcee jacket, which in classic lounge-singer fashion, was casually draped over his shoulder.

"Hello, Buck," said Noah, rising to greet him.

"Congratulations again, Noah," Buck said, offering his hand. "That was one fine speech you gave. Very inspired. Something everyone will carry with them for a long time to come."

"Thanks. It came from the heart." Noah drew Leviticus toward him with a fatherly grip on the arm. "You remember my boy, don't you?"

"Of course. Leviticus, a blessing to see you."

"A blessing to see you, Buck."

Then Leviticus noticed the button affixed to Verily's ruffled shirt.

An angry lamb.

Red lettering beneath: BOL.

"Got it at the Blood of the Lamb party," said Verily, looking down at his shirt. "They're really throwing a bash. All sorts of freebies. And . . ." he reached into the pocket of his suit and removed a bulky napkin, the unwrapping of which revealed something resembling a thick pork chop, " . . . great food!"

Leviticus glanced at his father, and at their own paltry offerings. He shut his eyes. Man does not live . . .

"Well, man doesn't live by bread alone," said Noah.

"I don't believe these are breaded," Buck said, poking at the chop. "Some type of sauce on it, but not breading by any stretch of the imagination."

"How many awards did they win tonight?" Noah asked defensively.

"None, but they sure are making an impact, aren't they?"

Enough of an impact that Leviticus abandoned the Good Samaritan party, telling his father that he was going to track down Evie. While it was accurate that he did want to locate his sister, his real mission was to do some reconnaissance at the BOL party. It wasn't hard to find. He just followed the crowds.

Word had spread rapidly through the believers at the Dixie Deluxe Inn, and when Leviticus arrived at the string of suites on the other end of the building he realized that pork chops were only part of the good news. The menu included barbecued beef and steak kabobs and salmon. Not to mention the mound of fresh fruit and a fabulous array of desserts and a staggering variety of nonalcoholic drinks. Leviticus resisted the temptation to partake. He wasn't about to break bread with Blood of the Lamb.

In addition to the food, there was entertainment. Doug Hosannah had been recruited, and he stood in the corner doing sleight-of-hand tricks. Over in the other corner a three-piece polka band was serenading the guests with familiar hymns.

An undercurrent in the crowd washed Leviticus toward another table, this one stacked with bumper stickers, buttons, and various promotional materials, carrying a mix of antiabortion sentiments and advertisements for BOL films.

Then Leviticus noticed that the walls in the party room were lined with lurid movie posters. *Babykiller* showed a brutish physician and a simple question: WAS HE A DOCTOR OR A MADMAN? *Die, Baby, Die!* depicted a frightened fetus with no mother in sight (no wonder he was afraid, Leviticus thought), cowering from the long glistening needle poised above his or her head. Even the innocuous-sounding *Debbie's Choice* had a less-than-innocent poster: an extremely pregnant teenager with another leering, thick-eyebrowed doctor looming godlike above her, and another question: WAS IT A CHOICE OR COLD-BLOODED MURDER?

The next poster Leviticus tried to inspect was blocked by Grant Godlee.

Leviticus waved to the host of the former *Quiet Hour Theater,* and the pair met somewhere near the middle of the room.

"Didn't expect to see you here," said Godlee, who had a BOL angry lamb button affixed to an otherwise clean white shirt.

"I was looking for my sister, actually."

"Haven't seen her, I'm afraid," said Godlee. He removed a napkin from his pocket and unfurled it. Nibbling on the bone, he said, "Have you tried the pork chops? They're wonderful."

"They're probably from a fetal pig."

Godlee laughed. "Good one."

"You look pretty happy," Leviticus said.

"I am. Nothing personal, but the arrangement with the Blood of the Lamb folks has really been a blessing."

"I hope for your sake the quality of the films has improved. I wouldn't want to sit through that junk every week."

Godlee took the jab seriously. "Actually, you're quite right. Good Samaritan's films were far superior in terms of the technical aspects. But the Blood of the Lamb features have a certain raw energy."

"Very raw," said Leviticus.

"I know they're looking to upgrade their product in all areas. The scripts, especially. They want to touch a wide audience, and they're not going to do it by making simple shock films. At the moment they have a surplus of passion and devotion, but not enough artistry."

"I wonder if they'll be around long enough to achieve that. Somehow I don't think a Nathaniel Berea Award is in their future."

"I should get down to the Good Samaritan suite and congratulate your father," said Grant. "How was the crowd there?"

"You won't have any trouble finding a place to sit."

It appeared as if the BOL party room was beginning to thin out, too. People were filing at a steady clip through a door along the side wall, leading to an adjacent suite.

"What's going on in there?" Leviticus wondered aloud.

"I heard they're having a funeral for the fetus," Godlee said matter-of-factly.

"The fetus?" Leviticus asked with a puzzled look. "You mean from the magic show?"

"Do you know of another fetus that was in attendance tonight?"

"But that wasn't real. I mean, it couldn't have been. . . . "

Godlee shrugged.

"Are you going to go?" Leviticus asked him.

"Well, I probably should put in an appearance. Do you want to go, too?"

"No, I don't want to go. I have to . . ." Leviticus glanced longingly at the exit, " . . . find my sister."

"You could just go for a minute. Poke your head in and so forth."

"You can tell me about it later."

"I don't plan on staying long myself," said Godlee, moving for the inner door. "Just long enough to pay my respects."

Leviticus headed for the door that would take him away from the Blood of the Lamb party, but before he left he passed by a food table and quickly sneaked a pork chop, wrapping it in a napkin and stuffing it into his pocket.

While walking by the half-closed doors leading to the main ball-room, Leviticus paused, hearing voices. The doors swung open, and there stood Evie, teary-eyed, coming out of the ballroom with a strange man in a blue blazer, his blond hair cropped short. Where have I seen that blazer before? Leviticus wondered.

She shook the stranger's hand gratefully, nodded, then spotted her brother.

"What are you doing here?" she asked, looking at him oddly. "Why aren't you at the party?"

"Is this the one then?" inquired the man in the blue blazer.

"No, this is just my brother. I'm okay now. Thanks for your help."

"You're welcome. And good luck to you, ma'am."

Leviticus watched the blue blazer depart, then returned his gaze to Evie. "Who was that?"

She glanced away. "Just someone I met." Now she looked back at him, challenge in her eyes. "I'm allowed to meet people, aren't I? Or would I be ruining Good Samaritan's image if I did that?"

"No, of course not. The way you were talking, though, it seemed a little personal."

"Well, maybe it was."

Leviticus remembered where he had seen the blue blazers be-fore. The counselors at the conclusion of the Ark Awards. Those who took the walk talked to the counselors, who gave them advice and information on what step to take next to ensure they were on the proper spiritual path.

"You didn't stand up at the end and accept anything," Leviticus said. "You were sitting at the table like the rest of us. I didn't see you afterward. You must have waited until we all left."

Evie looked at her brother for a long time, her expression increasingly pained, then she came to him and they embraced. "Oh, Leviticus," she said, breathing fast, "I'm in such bad trouble."

"I knew something was up."

"I'm sorry I didn't come to you right away. But our family doesn't always work the best, we don't always see things so clearly. I needed someone to talk to, someone who was on the outside."

Leviticus broke the hug so that he could see her face. "What's going on, Evie? What happened?"

She glanced up and down the hallway. A few people were ambling by, chatting and laughing. "Not here," she said. "Let's go outside."

Brother and sister went out to meet a chilly winter's night in Virginia. They walked across the parking lot of the hotel, sitting down on a curb in a distant corner. The lights of Lynchburg shone in the distance, like headlights at a hanging.

"What's that odor?" Evie asked. "It smells like . . ."

"Pork chop," Leviticus finished. "I was hungry." He removed the chop from his pocket and nibbled on it, thinking that it tasted more like lamb than pork.

They sat quietly for a time, in the night, and Leviticus began thinking. Have I been a good brother to Evie? he wondered. He sensed that she needed things from him on an emotional level that he didn't grasp. He wanted to help her. Four years ago she was hurt in a car accident, and he had stayed at her bedside nearly continuously until she was released from the hospital. But in an accident of the heart, he didn't know what to do. It was hard to talk about emotions. He felt frustrated, and finally said, "It's good to get out of there. So much wild partying. I don't think I could take more than one of these a year."

Evie rested her chin on her knees, arms wrapped tight around her legs.

"Have you and Rick broken up?" Leviticus asked her suddenly.

She slowly turned her head toward him, and then began laughing.

"What did I say? What's so funny?"

She touched his arm, her eyes tear-filled again. "No, we haven't broken up. We should have, we really should have, but now it's . . . too late."

"Too late for what?"

Taking his hands in her own, Evie told him softly, "Leviticus, I'm pregnant."

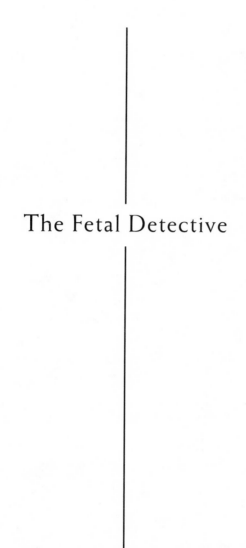

The Fetal Detective

Eighteen

THE SLUSH PILE AT *CHRISTIAN BUS DRIVER* MAGAZINE HAD GROWN into a mountain as high as the sins of the unredeemed. This used to be Rosemary's responsibility, to find those rare jewels that would enlighten and entertain all bus drivers in the Lord everywhere. But she was at the seminary now, and her replacement, Nicholas Puckett, while a friendly and talented young man, didn't appear to have the most essential quality found in all good editorial assistants: the ability to toil steadily on monotonous tasks. More than once Bob Countenance had caught him working on his own writing when there was work for the magazine to be done, and deadlines to meet. Hopefully it was just a matter of him settling into the new job. Until then, until Bob felt that he could trust Nicholas' editorial judgment, he decided to assume the burden of the slush pile himself. He kept Nicholas busy with proofreading.

Although the mound of unsolicited manuscripts was great, Bob's long experience in the inspirational magazine business, including stints at *Christian Dental Hygienist* and *Christian Cement-Mixer Truck Driver* magazines, would see him through. It gave him the ability to spot an unsuitable article by the end of the first page, and often by the time he finished the first paragraph.

It wasn't that the articles were poorly written; in fact, most of them were quite adequate in that regard. The problem was that the

majority of these prospective writers had not bothered to contact
the magazine for its editorial guidelines, so they had no clue as to
Christian Bus Driver's mission. Many of the submissions were inappropriate at best.

Take the one Bob had just tossed into the reject pile, "Driving
in Satan's Fast Lane." The piece contained worthy sentiments about
living a life of modesty and dedication to God, but it offered no
practical advice to the magazine's readers. Like what prayers to say
before starting on your route. Or fifteen ways to avoid taking the
Lord's name in vain when the kids are causing a ruckus.

Other articles were perfectly appropriate but lacking in rele-
vance or common sense. Some of these raised questions about their
status as nonfiction. Bob barely had to read beyond the titles on
these: "I Picked Up an Angel"; "Dashboard Jesus Saves Family of
Five"; "Satan in My Master Cylinder".

So Bob spent a good hour paring the slush pile down to a man-
ageable height, then checked in on Nicholas before heading to
lunch and the post office.

His new staff member was hunched over the keyboard in his
cramped yet perfectly adequate cubicle, typing frenetically.

"All done proofing for the day, are you?"

Nick stopped typing, then looked up sheepishly. "Not quite."
He picked up the manuscript and flipped the pages back and forth,
apparently forgetting where he had left off reading.

Bob mentally rattled off fifteen ways of taking the Lord's name
in vain when the editorial assistant isn't doing his job. "Listen,
Nicholas, I think I'm a pretty easygoing boss. I don't mind if you
work on your own writing if you find yourself with some spare moments. Certain times of the month are slower than others, we all
know that. But the editorial deadline for the March issue is next
Thursday, and we've got a pile of articles that need to be proofed
and typeset." Bob took the manuscript from Nick's hands. It was
the lead piece for March, "How to Respond to Those Child-
Molestation Rumors."

Handing the pages back to his assistant, Bob thought of fifteen ways to fire his sorry God-fearing posterior, then said in a calm voice, "I gave this to you to proof first thing this morning. Here it is almost noon and you haven't finished it."

"Sorry."

Bob forgave him immediately, of course, but that didn't assuage his concerns. "This is an important article, one of the more controversial things we've ever done at *Christian Bus Driver*. People are going to be reading the magazine a lot more carefully than they normally would. We have to make sure everything is in pristine shape. You don't want us to look bad, do you?"

"No, of course not."

Now a great peacefulness descended over Bob Countenance. He gave Nick a friendly look. "Well, do your best, all right? What were you working on anyway?"

He shrugged. "Just my stuff. I'm almost done. That's why I got distracted. Once I'm done with it, I'll do better."

"Can I look at it when you're finished?"

"It's probably not very good."

"You should try writing an article for the magazine sometime. I'd pay you the same rate as any other freelancer."

"Really?"

"Absolutely." Bob left the office, figuring that if the boy was going to be working on extracurricular writing projects, it may as well be in the service of the magazine.

Bob picked up the tidy bundle of mail at the post office and went to lunch at the neighborhood Fat Boy. The usual solicitations, proposals, and bills. Another missive from Mrs. Bearman. She was a regular correspondent to the magazine. Her husband had driven a bus for an evangelical school for many years before his death in a hunting accident. Her letters tended to be long and disjointed, but Bob found them entertaining in a strange way and usually printed them. The only time he had refused to run one of her letters was when she wrote a long essay retelling the Easter story.

It had no opinions or personal impressions, which was a definite liability for a piece meant for the letters column. He wrote her back explaining why he couldn't run it, and then several months passed before she forgave and forgot and resumed her correspondence.

Her current submission was anorexic by comparison, judging by the envelope. Not even a two-stamper. Bob sliced it open and pulled out the letter.

It was her briefest contribution ever. Bob didn't know if that meant it was more significant or if she simply was too busy to ramble on at her usual length.

It said:

> *Dear Bob,*
>
> *Why are the bus drivers getting so mean?*
>
> > *Yours in Christ,*
> >
> > *Mrs. Bearman*

Bob wasn't exactly sure what she was getting at, but decided to print it anyway, just to keep their relationship off the road to alienation. When Bob returned from lunch, he stopped in at Nicholas' cubicle, finding the molestation article in more or less the same spot as when he left. Shaking his head, Bob scooped up the pages, squaring them on the edge of the desk. He moved the mouse, getting rid of the screen savior. After scrolling backward for a dozen pages or so, Bob glanced over his shoulder, then got to work. He closed the file, copied it to a floppy disk, reopened the document at the point where he had discovered it, and stole back to his own office. If it's on my time, it's my business, he thought, shutting his door.

Later, Bob returned to his new assistant's office, and found the boy anxiously riffling through papers scattered across his desk.

"Looking for something?" Bob asked, dangling the molestation manuscript before him.

Nick's eyes darted from the article to Bob and back again, and then he sat down in a heap. "Whew, I thought I lost it." He took it from Bob's hand, saying, "From now on, it's all business. I finished what I was working on. You've got me one hundred and ten percent of the time from now on. I promise."

"I didn't know you wanted to write stories."

Nick got a funny look on him.

"It was an accident," Bob said, not sounding apologetic. "Somehow I got the wrong file onto my computer. You know how computers are."

"I'm really sorry, Mr. Countenance."

"Don't be." He looked admiringly at Nick. "You're a very clever writer, son. It's not exactly something I'd go for personally, but I know good writing when I see it."

"Gosh. Thanks."

"Do you have plans to submit it anywhere?"

He shrugged. "I kind of thought about it. But I didn't know if it was any good."

"Well, you do know that one of our columnists, Leviticus Speck, is an executive at a very highly respected inspirational film company. I don't think it's something they'd want to produce, but he is a professional and he might be able to give you some pointers."

"That would be more than amazing, Mr. Countenance. Good Samaritan. Rance Jericho. Whew."

"I'll give him a call this afternoon."

"Leviticus, this is Bob Countenance."

"Well, good afternoon to you, Bob. It's a blessing to hear from you. I'm sorry I haven't gotten my column in yet, but with the Arks and everything . . ."

"No problem. As soon as you're able. What's it about?"

"A recap of the Arks. First person, You Are There sort of approach."

"Sounds fine. Say, pass my congratulations along to Noah. That was quite an honor. He's really had a blessed life."

"I'll tell him you called."

"There was something else I wanted to talk to you about, Leviticus."

"Fire away."

"Well, it's about my new editorial assistant, Nicholas Puckett. I told you about him, didn't I?"

"I remember you mentioning him, but beyond that I have to admit I don't recall what you said. You'll have to forgive me."

"I do. Nicholas is quite a talented writer. He showed me something he wrote. I was wondering if I could impose on you by asking you to read it, and give him your feedback. I'd consider it a personal favor, Leviticus."

"Go ahead and send it over, Bob. Just to warn you, though, I'm not going to have a lot of time to spend on it."

"I'm sure he'd be thrilled with whatever you'd give him."

"By the way, what's it about?"

"It's a murder mystery, a Christian murder mystery."

Nineteen

IT HAD BEEN A QUIET SUMMER, RELAXING LIKE THE SLOW WAVES
of amniotic fluid, when I first got wind of the killings. I was in my
third trimester, and had been on my first case less than a week. A
Baby John Doe. Preborn. It wasn't pretty.

The mutilated body was discovered in a trash bin outside a
hospital. After some snooping around in the medical records department, I narrowed the list of suspects to one: a Dr. Henry Hacker.

I found the good doctor in his office. Threw some pictures on
his desk. Two weeks, four weeks, six weeks.

"Look familiar?" I asked him.

The only thing he looked for was a way out of the room.

"Don't try anything," I said. "I'm viable."

"I don't recognize him," he said.

"Take a real good look, pal."

"I tell you I don't recognize him. They all look alike to me."

His answer hit me like the hurricane of a vacuum aspirator.

"So this isn't the first time you've been involved in murder."

"No, I didn't mean that. I see a lot of fetuses. You forget faces
after a while. They don't really develop distinctive features until the
third trimester. They don't even have fingerprints until the ninth
week."

How convenient.

He was hiding something, that much I could tell. I slapped him around some until he spilled.

"Look, look," he said, "this was a spontaneous abortion. The mother was having health problems. . . ."

"Listen, mister, I saw the body. There was nothing spontaneous about it. It was cold-blooded murder. . . ."

Twenty

WHEN THE THICK MANILA ENVELOPE FROM *CHRISTIAN BUS DRIVER* magazine arrived at Good Samaritan, Leviticus looked at it for a moment, puzzled, then groaned silently when he remembered his conversation with Bob Countenance earlier in the week. He wished he hadn't agreed to critique the manuscript. His plate was already full. Elijah Winds had begged off returning to Virginia to shoot the footage at Holy Land USA, so Noah volunteered Leviticus for the job. He was busy making arrangements for that trip, as well as trying to round up extras at Coon Rapids Community College for a crowd scene in *Heaven Needs You!*, the sequel to *Hear the Word Again!*

However, a promise was a promise, and Bob was a friend of the family. Besides, he didn't expect Leviticus to give the manuscript more than a perfunctory glance.

Leviticus undid the clasp on the envelope, turned back the flap, and removed the contents.

> THE FETAL DETECTIVE
> (A Pro-Life Mystery)
> by Nicholas Puckett

This shouldn't take long, he thought.

Turning over the cover page, Leviticus began to read.

It had been a quiet summer. . . .

Leviticus kept reading, more slowly and carefully as he went on, and by the time he had flipped over the last page he fully understood the implications of what he held in his hands.

The next time I visited the doctor I brought along a good friend. He had a snub nose, but I don't pick my friends by their looks.

Caught the murderer red-handed, injecting saline solution into the amniotic sac. I shared the pain.

"Hold it right there, Doc."

But we both knew I was too late.

He had a long needle, but there's nothing like a good friend when you're in a jam.

Blam, blam, blam.

The only viable thing left in the room was yours truly.

So long, Doc. Have a nice trip to hell.

Some things you just know in your gut are trouble.

As Bob Countenance had correctly stated, *The Fetal Detective* was a little rough around the edges. It wasn't a work of genius. But it had a certain style, a sense of swagger, that lifted it above hack work, that gave it a very special quality. It may have been propaganda, but it was also most definitely art.

If Blood of the Lamb ever got their hands on this, Leviticus worried, it might be all over. This could give them legitimacy. They could get attention from the secular press. They would be taken seriously. And combined with their promotional savvy . . . Leviticus felt a chill zigzag down his spine.

He wanted to talk to the author, this Nicholas Puckett. Find out what his intentions were.

Was he as stridently pro-life as *The Fetal Detective* made him appear? Or was he just a slick marketer who knew how to pander to his audience? But if he wanted to sell to Blood of the Lamb, why did Good Samaritan end up with the manuscript?

Did Nicholas know what he had?

Unlikely. He was probably a kid in his twenties. Maybe his first job out of school. Living in a small city in Iowa. What could he know about the machinations of the inspirational film community?

Only one way to determine exactly what he did know. Leviticus picked up the phone, then set it back down. This call is very important, he thought. It's going to set in motion a relationship. If I take the wrong approach, say the wrong things, the game will be lost before it even begins.

Leviticus put on his overcoat and galoshes and stopped in at his dad's office. "I'm going to get some fresh air," he said. "I'll be back in a little bit."

"Watch the ice, son."

"I'll be careful."

Have to be very careful, Leviticus told himself, heading out the door into the biting January air. He thought about telling his father, showing him *The Fetal Detective*, but he was afraid it would be futile. Dad wouldn't take the time to read it. He was preoccupied with his own future these days. Even if he did read it, he wouldn't realize the implications. He was stubborn and single-minded. If Dad wouldn't help, Leviticus decided, then he must be kept completely out of the loop.

Leviticus headed across the narrow parking lot to the street. There were no sidewalks in the industrial park, so he walked on the left side of the street and kept shifting his gaze from the road ahead to the road surface. He was filled with anxiety. He knew he had to take action, and quickly, but he didn't know what to do.

Maybe I'm crazy, he thought. One strange story won't change the world. Let's say the worst possible scenario occurs, and Blood of the Lamb somehow gets hold of *The Fetal Detective* and brings it to life. So what? People see it and are either inspired or appalled or bored and then they move on. It won't change the world. It won't change anything. It's only a movie.

But these reasonable assurances didn't take the edge off the feeling in his heart, which was shot with dread.

Who else could he trust? Evie? He hadn't talked with her much since they returned from Lynchburg. Her pregnancy wasn't evident yet. The news had sent him reeling, although he didn't know why he should be surprised, considering all he knew about her relationship with Rick Bible, which apparently wasn't as much as he thought. He didn't want to add to her burdens. In quieter times, he would have made Evie's situation his first priority, but these weren't quiet times.

Leviticus kept walking, hunching down in the wind, hearing the creak of brittle branches from trees that were spared the bulldozer's blade.

Elijah?

No. He'd want to make the movie himself.

Leviticus stopped.

It was dangerous.

It could backfire.

It could be the only answer.

He hurried back to the office, bucking the wind, but somehow it didn't feel quite as frigid.

"Bob, hi, this is Leviticus Speck. How are you doing this afternoon?"

"Fine, Leviticus. It's a blessing to hear from you again."

"Super. Say, I need to talk to this assistant of yours, Nicholas Puckett."

"You've read the story, then. What did you think of it? Did you like it?"

"How long have you been hiding him from me, Bobby? He's a real find, a big talent."

"Why, that's wonderful. But this isn't the type of movie Good Samaritan can make . . . is it?"

"Put Nicholas on the phone. I'd like to tell him myself."

Seconds later:

"Hi, this is Nicholas."

"Nick, Leviticus Speck, Good Samaritan Films."

"Hi."

"Nick, your boss there, Mr. Countenance, took the liberty of sending me a copy of your story, *The Fetal Detective*. You're the author of this work, right?"

"I sure am. I got into trouble because I was writing it during business hours. You can ask Mr. Countenance."

"Well, Nick, I read it this morning, and I wanted to call and tell you I liked it. I liked it a lot, as a matter of fact. Especially the part where the detective bombs the health clinic where all the bad guys are hiding out."

"Whew."

"Now, I'm not saying it's perfect. And we do need to get it into screenplay format."

"I've never written a screenplay before," Nick confessed.

"Don't worry about it. Any talented writer can handle it, and you have talent to spare. There are a few sections that need to be shored up, but I think it's something we can work with. It's something we'd be interested in working on with *you*. How does that sound?"

"I don't believe this is happening."

"How soon could you fly in for a meeting?"

"A meeting? Gosh, I don't know. The magazine. Mr. Countenance."

"I'm sure he'll give you the time off. We'll pay for everything, the flight, the hotel, your meals."

"Hang on. I'll ask him. . . . How about Friday? I can be there on Friday."

"Perfect. I'll call you back once everything is set up. The studio's been pretty crazy lately; we're working on new versions of Rance Jericho's classic Savior films from the fifties and sixties. So we're going to bring you in and turn you around and shoot you back home pretty quickly so you can get started on the script. I just mention it so you don't feel like we're trying to get rid of you. It's a hurry-up business. In that way, at least, we're a lot like Hollywood."

"I'm a big fan of Rance Jericho. They showed us all his movies when I was a kid in Sunday school back in North Dakota. Is he still alive?"

"He's alive and doing great. Would you like to meet him?"

"Are you kidding?"

"He's a friend. Won't be a problem. I'll take care of everything. You're my guy, Nick."

It was a big city. With a lot of doctors.

There was work to be done.

I gave my friend with the snub nose a rest. Called up another friend, one with a short fuse.

I broke the window to one of their hideouts. Lit the fuse and tossed it in.

This one's for the kids. . . .

Twenty-One

LEVITICUS WAS CONFUSED, AND THERE WAS ONLY ONE PERSON HE turned to when he was confused and that was the man who played the Lord in the movies.

But he hadn't spoken with Rance since last summer, hadn't seen him face-to-face in a year.

He wasn't sure how he expected Rance to help. In part, it was Nicholas' admiration for the film legend that prompted this unannounced visit. There was a connection, and Leviticus was desperately in search of connections. Beyond that was the fact that Leviticus had no one else to turn to. Rance was family, but separated family. He could be objective. Leviticus trusted his judgment, and they had gotten along well before the fallout.

Over everything, though, loomed Rance Jericho's persona as the Savior. When Leviticus said his prayers at night, the image in his mind was the fatherly visage of Rance Jericho. He knew it was ridiculous and probably morally wrong, but the myth had a stronger claim on Leviticus than rational thought. His upbringing was in film, more than the church, and in film—inspirational cinema—was where his deepest loyalties and faith lay.

Leviticus slowed, pulling his car into Rance's driveway. He trudged up the ice-encrusted sidewalk and rang the bell.

The door swung open. "So, the prodigal film executive returns," Rance said in a slightly slurred voice.

"Hey, Rance," said Leviticus. "You're looking great."

"I feel like hell. Come on in."

"Sorry I haven't been in touch."

A trio of beer bottles were lined up like bowling pins on the coffee table, an opened case hugged the television. Rance plopped down on the couch. Leviticus didn't join him. Judging by his reception, he didn't think he would be staying long. "You heard about Rick Bible, didn't you?"

"The King of King of Kings. I'm glad I wasn't wasting my breath."

"You did a wonderful job with him, Rance. Elijah said half that Ark belongs to you."

"Not much of a future for a Christ trainer, though. One per generation is usually plenty." Rance reached for the nearest brown bottle. It fell over on the table, spinning around slowly.

Rance stared at it. "I know, we could do a remake of *The Bottle or the Lord*. Only this time I'll play the Savior as an alcoholic. That way, your dad would be happy and I'd be able to stretch myself as an actor." Stopping the bottle with his hand, Rance looked at the younger Speck. "Whaddya say, Leviticus? Do you think there's an audience for a film like that?"

Leviticus had never seen Rance in this state, and he found it quite disturbing. It made him feel like whatever pinions held up the world were rotting away, and soon they all would tumble into the abyss. It was as if God turned out to be made of papier-mâché. Leviticus wanted to leave. He wanted to give up and get a job in a bank.

But he didn't move or say anything.

"Look, Leviticus," Rance finally said, his voice soft and sober, "I'm not the same man you remember. Things have changed. My life has changed. I put away the robe and sandals for good, and passed the cross to a younger man. I feel like a large part of me has died. Only the rest of me has to go on living, and no matter what

I try, I can't rise again. Nobody pushed the stone away, and even if they did, I don't know what I'd do once I came out into the light again."

Leviticus gazed at his idol for a long moment. "There's trouble," he said. "Good Samaritan's in trouble. Dad doesn't realize it or won't admit it. I don't know what to do. I . . . I didn't know who else to turn to."

"What kind of trouble?"

Leviticus told him about the laughter in Tarzana, the demise of *Quiet Hour Theater*, and what he knew about Blood of the Lamb and the future they were creating. He told him about *The Fetal Detective*, too, and what he thought would happen if the competition got their bloody hands on it.

"I need your help," said Leviticus. "I told the author that we're interested in making a movie based on his story. He's flying into town on Friday. He's a fan of yours. I told him I'd introduce him to you."

"You're not actually planning to make this movie, this *Fetal Detective*, then."

Leviticus shook his head. "I had to buy myself some time. I didn't know what else to do."

"And when he finds out that you have no intention of making the film?"

"I don't know."

Rance stood up unsteadily. "I hope you're not appealing to my sense of loyalty to Good Samaritan, because I have very little at this point."

"I don't know what I'm appealing to," said Leviticus. "You certainly don't owe me any favors. It's just that I've looked up to you for so many years in a religious sort of way and I was kind of wishing for . . ."

"An act of God?"

Leviticus nodded self-consciously, not looking at Rance.

"I can't live up to those expectations anymore, son. I left that behind when I passed my robe and sandals to Rick. You're not looking at me for who I am."

Leviticus returned his gaze to Rance. "How about as a favor to a friend?"

"As a friend," said Rance, sitting down again, craggy hands on his lap. "As a friend, I would help you."

Leviticus no longer felt alone. He said a silent prayer, thanking God for delivering unto him a friend.

"What do you want me to do?" Rance asked. "Shake the kid's hand and tell him a few stories about the good old days? Give him an autographed photo? Show him my awards?"

"All that would be fine," said Leviticus, "but there's something else I'd like you to do, too. . . ."

Twenty-Two

THE FATHER OF THE FETAL DETECTIVE WAS COMING TO TOWN.

Leviticus told his own dad that he was going to take a long lunch, then drove down to the airport. After parking his car, Leviticus scrawled PUCKETT on a legal pad and hurried into the terminal.

The flight from Iowa arrived on schedule, and in a short time the passengers disembarked. Leviticus didn't spot the slender, dark-eyed young man until they were looking at one another eye to eye.

"Hi. I'm Nick."

Trying to cover his surprise, Leviticus offered his hand. "A pleasure to meet you, Nick. I'm Leviticus Speck."

"It's an honor."

What surprised Leviticus was the appearance of Nicholas Puckett. He had been expecting the standard-issue twentysomething, scrubbed-to-a-shine contemporary Christian look. Either that or the "alternative" young Christian look: untucked flannel shirts, facial hair, sullen expressions. Only the flannel shirts were a bit too smartly pressed, the facial hair resembled the beard on a Ken doll, and the sullen expressions were set on faces that were a touch too well fed.

However, even though Nick was dressed in a white shirt and dark slacks, was clean-shaven and even sported a gold crucifix around his neck, he looked slightly dangerous. Not dangerous in the Ricky Bible, girl-chasing, fast-driving sense. Dangerous in a new way that Leviticus had never encountered in a Christian before. Dangerous in a Fetal Detective way, whatever that might turn out to mean.

"Let's get your luggage," said Leviticus, as they walked back through the terminal.

"This is it," Nick said, patting his small black shoulder bag.

"Great. I'll take you right to your hotel then."

Leviticus set up his guest at the Pilot Knob Plaza. He used his personal credit card to pay for the room, not wanting anything unusual to show up on a Good Samaritan account. They rode the elevator to the fourth floor. "I thought you'd like a chance to settle in and so forth before we get started. We can eat dinner later and then stop in at Rance Jericho's place."

"Sounds great."

"Why don't we meet in the restaurant downstairs at six?"

"Okay."

So Leviticus saw Nick to his room, then returned to work for the balance of the afternoon, made another excuse for his evening absence, and headed back to the hotel.

Nick was waiting for him in the nautically themed café, in a corner booth beneath a picturesque painting of a whale harpooning.

Sliding into the booth, Leviticus greeted his guest, noticing that he was absently flipping the pages of a Bible with his thumb. Nick saw where he was looking and said, glancing about, "I found it in the drawer in my room. I want Mr. Jericho to autograph it. Do you think he'll do it?"

Leviticus wasn't sure if he was joking or not, so he didn't know if he should just laugh and move on or attempt to answer the question sincerely. "Well, I'm not sure," Leviticus said slowly. "I guess it wouldn't hurt to ask."

"Cool."

After they had ordered and were waiting for the food to arrive, Leviticus said, "So let's talk a little about *The Fetal Detective.*"

"Sure."

"It's certainly an unusual idea."

"Is it? Maybe it is. I don't know. I get a lot of ideas."

A lot of ideas. "How did you get this one?" Leviticus asked him.

His eyes shone, and he sat forward. "I had a . . . vision."

The word chilled Leviticus. "A vision," he repeated.

"Yeah, it was weird. There's this billboard on the way to work, I see it every day. A giant fetus, all golden and perfect, with the words: A CHOICE OR A CHILD? I got to thinking about it, how the way it looks on the billboard, the fetus is a separate person. You can't even tell there's a mother surrounding it. And the posture, something struck me as really odd about the posture. Something was being suggested, not a choice or a child, but something more. Only I couldn't figure out what."

Leviticus sipped his ice water. "What was odd about it?"

"Well, I wondered the same thing until one day last spring when I drove by it and saw that the picture had changed. The fetus was wearing a fedora, and it was packing heat. Looked like a snub-nosed revolver. I don't know guns that well. And it had an expression on its face, sort of a combination of world-weariness and righteous anger."

Did he look like an angry lamb? Leviticus wondered.

"It was clear to me that the fetus was a detective."

What else could he be?

"But the next day when I drove by the billboard it had returned to normal, if that's what normal was."

"So the fetal detective goes around solving crimes against the unborn."

"Yes," said Nick. "Mostly murders, since that's the number one crime worry among the preborn."

It was a standoff at the reproductive canal. The "doctors" were armed with a saline-filled syringe and a vacuum aspirator that looked like it meant business. All

I had was my best friend and a pair of bare fists that were itching to meet up with the jaws of some medical men.

Word about my exploits had gotten around town. I had been stepping on a lot of big toes the past few weeks. I was a marked fetus. They figured they could gang up on me and finish me off before I broke up their little racket for good. Well, I thought, come on in and get me, Docs. Let's dance.

I figured they would be storming in the usual way, the easy way. They always look for the easy way. I knew they wouldn't do anything to endanger the mother's health. Not the mother's health.

Then I got a hunch. It had been quiet for a while, apart from the contractions occurring at regular intervals, which meant something. They were scared. Otherwise, they would have waltzed right up the repo canal and crushed my skull.

The quiet meant something, so I played my hunch.

I turned my attention away from the repo canal. I aimed my best pal right at the spot where I figured the incision would be made, and lay very still.

When they performed that C-section, I would be waiting.

In a short time the food came, Leviticus with the roasted chicken, a vegetarian pizza for Nick.

"I was going to ask you what your views on abortion are," Leviticus said, rending drumstick from thigh, "but I guess I've got a pretty clear idea now."

"Does it matter?"

"Well, yes, it does matter. As you probably know, Nick, *The Fetal Detective* would be quite a departure for Good Samaritan. Not that we don't need a new direction; we're in a bit of a rut, that's for sure. But we would want to make sure that we're all reading from the same page of Scripture, as it were."

The author shrugged, stuffing pizza into his mouth. "Whatever."

"Do you think life begins at conception?"

"I don't know. To be honest, Mr. Speck, I didn't do a lot of research before I started writing. It all just sort of came together as I wrote it."

Leviticus felt some relief. Nick was no Blood of the Lamb disciple. At least not yet. But if a story like this was the product of an uncommitted mind, what would happen if he took up the cause? Leviticus wanted to change the subject, get things on the upbeat side again.

"I'd like to start shooting *The Fetal Detective* as soon as possible," said Leviticus. "We have a standard contract, I'm sure you'll find it more than fair. We're scheduled to do some location shooting in Virginia shortly. We'll set you up in a hotel and you can work on the script right there." Leviticus slowly moved his hands in an arc. "I've got it all blocked out in my mind. It'll be beautiful. A work of art. We'll do your vision justice, Nick, that I vow to you."

"Cool. Who's going to play the detective?"

Leviticus smiled. "Finish your dinner and I'll introduce you to him."

Twenty-Three

THEY SKIPPED DESSERT, CHOOSING THE SPIRIT OVER THE SHERBET.

When they arrived at the Jericho residence, Leviticus rang the doorbell, noticing as he did that the shades were drawn on all the windows. It was quiet as a congregation.

"I'm pretty nervous," said Nick, fidgeting on the bottom step. "I've never met anyone so famous. It's like going to heaven or something."

"Don't worry," Leviticus said. "I feel like that myself sometimes."

The door didn't open, but a booming voice from inside bade them to enter.

Leviticus glanced back. "Shall we?"

They crossed the threshold into the dark cool house and found themselves face-to-face not with the legendary Christus but the living incarnation of a more modern hero.

Nick was staring wide-eyed, and Leviticus grinned in amazement. Rance had really gone all out. Gray trench coat and fedora (hair tucked neatly under the brim), a revolver, and no mercy. On the wall behind him, illuminated by a spotlight in the ceiling, a glowing golden fetus in poster form oversaw the proceedings.

Rance peered at them with a mix of world-weariness and righteous anger, and said, *"The next time I visited the doctor I brought along a good friend. He had a snub nose, but I don't pick my friends by their looks.*

Caught the murderer red-handed, injecting saline solution into the amniotic sac. I shared the pain."

Aiming the gun at an unseen target, Rance said, *"Hold it right there, Doc."*

A long moment passed. It was a standoff.

Then Rance continued, *"But we both knew I was too late. He had a long needle, but there's nothing like a good friend when you're in a jam."*

Suddenly Rance squeezed the trigger, and the gun popped loudly three times. Both Leviticus and Nick flinched.

Rance returned the gun to its holster inside his coat. *"The only viable thing left in the room was yours truly,"* he said. *"So long, Doc. Have a nice trip to hell. . . ."* He paused, then tugged at his hat and walked over to the wall, making the room dark.

When the lights came up again, Leviticus saw that the kid had tears in his eyes. Rance removed his coat and hat and came over to them.

"That was beautiful, Mr. Jericho," said Nick. "Just like I pictured it. What an honor to hear you read my words. I've been a big fan of yours, like forever."

"Acting is so much easier with well-written dialogue," Rance said, clasping his admirer's hand.

"Thanks. Thanks a lot." Shaking his head and laughing, Nick said, "Rance Jericho as the Fetal Detective. I can't believe it. I just can't believe it." He turned to Leviticus. "You weren't lying. You said you would do my work justice. You really meant it, didn't you?"

"Of course."

"I want to get started on the script right now."

"Absolutely."

"Geez, I almost forget," said Nick, heading for the door.

"Forgot?"

"I wanted to get Mr. Jericho's autograph. Don't go anywhere, okay?"

When the boy departed, Leviticus said to Rance, "You did a really fine job, Rance. First rate as always. The old pro. You're a class act."

"It felt good to be doing some real acting again," said Rance.

Nick returned, Gideon Bible in hand. Rance graciously signed his name, inscribing it, "For Nicholas, my colleague, Rance Jericho."

"This is the most exciting day of my life," said Nick, fingertips brushing the autographed page. "You were the King, you always will be the King to me. I remember seeing *Every Day is Christmas* at a church lock-in. It was the first time I witnessed you in action. I bet I've watched it fifty times since then."

"You are a man of distinctive tastes," said Rance. "I didn't think anyone even remembered that film. It hasn't been on television in years."

Every Day is Christmas told the tale of a mysterious stranger who arrives in the town of Gomorrah, Illinois, one Christmas Eve. He has long hair and speaks strangely. He rents a room and is seen doing odd jobs as a carpenter. A story spreads among the local kids that the man is really Jesus. He befriends the children and some of the town's less desirable characters. One day the stranger leaves as mysteriously as he appeared, and the town is changed forever by his loving example.

"But it's my favorite," said Nick. "You really made Him come alive."

Rance bowed graciously.

"I liked the others, too, especially the historical ones. When you died on the cross, I felt like I was right up there with you. What did it feel like, to die on a cross, even if it was just pretend?"

"Well, I think it gave me a unique insight into His suffering," said Rance. "We repeat the story so often that we remove ourselves from the reality of what happened. Even I found it hard to imagine what it must have been like to feel your life drain away with each throbbing second of agony. Of course, I could only glimpse the glory when that stone was rolled away and He rose again."

"You're the best, Mr. Jericho."

"God bless you, kid."

The plan to abort *The Fetal Detective* was set into motion. The next day Leviticus made two extra reservations for the trip to Virginia. It wasn't safe to keep Nick within range of the Good Samaritan headquarters. He might get a notion to stop by the offices without an appointment. The best bet was to bring him along to Virginia, keep him busy writing and gushing over Rance while Leviticus supervised the shooting at Holy Land USA.

Leviticus figured he could string young Nicholas along for a couple of months at least. After that, well, Leviticus had been praying for guidance on this matter every night since *The Fetal Detective* had dropped into his life.

Tonight was no different. After he had tucked in Nick back at the Pilot Knob and returned home, Leviticus traded his dress slacks and white shirt for his Bible-adorned pajamas. He knelt on the wooden floor in front of his bed and folded his hands. He didn't shut his eyes at first, gazing out the window at the Creator's tapestry. Then he closed off the world of flesh and sin, picturing Rance in the Good Samaritan production of *Hear the Word!*, and said this prayer:

Lord, I always try to do Thy will, but sometimes it's hard to know what to do. I don't want to lie to Nicholas or lead him on, I really don't. It's just that right now it seems like the lesser of two evils. Is there such a thing as the lesser of two evils, Lord? Am I just kidding myself? Should I let evil be with evil?

Leviticus stretched out his arms on the bed, head resting on them, hands still folded.

In my heart, Lord, I know that Nicholas has produced something that isn't good. The same way that Blood of the Lamb isn't good. They aren't about love. It's not that there isn't enough love, there is no love. They've replaced it with something else. Something I don't understand. Something I was never taught. Where did they learn this, Lord, from you? They couldn't have learned this from you, could they?

In any case, I need some guidance. I just want to do your will. I remain your humble servant. God bless Dad and Evie and Rick and Rance and Nick and Grant Godlee and even Paul Pedphill. And God bless all Good Samaritans everywhere. Amen.

Twenty-Four

WHEN EVIE FIRST DISCOVERED HER PREGNANCY, SHE WONDERED IF HER misgivings about being the partner of a Christus were misplaced. Some days she actually didn't feel like she was carrying the Savior's child. The creation germinating within was the byproduct of an actor and a film executive's deepest feelings, nothing more. The aura of Christus Rick terminated at her fallopian tubes. A pleasant surprise.

On other days, she fully felt as if she were nurturing the grandson of God inside her body.

Those were the days when she truly sensed the distance between herself and her man. She would go over to his apartment after work and listen to him recite his lines, her eyes closed, clutching her crucifix. He was too good, too believable. Then he would break out of character and chase her around the couch. He was Rick, but he was something else, too.

Evie yearned for someone to share her feelings with, but there was no one. Her family members were her closest friends. Dad was out of the question; he didn't even know she and Rick were dating. Leviticus seemed too emotional about the situation to offer any useful advice. Although Evie had acquaintances in the inspirational film community, she didn't think she wanted to bare her life before them. There was always that fellow at the Ark Awards, the counselor whom she first went to for help. She didn't know where to reach him, though, even if she could remember his name.

There was one other possibility. She considered it carefully. It made sense. He was nearly family, yet estranged from them. He had the right kind of experience. After all, he had helped create the new Rick Bible, so he should have some thoughts on how to live with his creation. Better yet, he and his ex-wife broke up over the very things she was worried about.

Rance Jericho would have the answers she was searching for.

"Evie, it's always a pleasure to see my little angel."

Rance had called her that since she was in grade school. She didn't mind. It reminded her of more innocent times.

"I'm sorry I haven't kept in touch better," she said, giving him a hug. "I feel sort of funny running to you for help now. I hope you don't think I'm being terribly selfish."

"Nothing could change my feelings about you," said Rance, leading her to the couch, where they sat down. "You have a precious heart. No matter what has happened between your father and me, you will always be dear to me."

Evie looked down, hands clasped. She had been afraid that she wouldn't recognize him, that the bitterness and the loss of his identity as the Christus had broken pieces from him. Maybe he had changed. He seemed a little gaunt, a little sad-eyed. However, she badly wanted to see the old Rance, to feel the comfort he could provide.

"You were rather vague on the phone," said Rance. "What's going on? You mentioned something about a problem with Ricky Bible."

She nodded. "I don't know if he told you anything about us. . . ."

"No, he didn't."

"Well, we've been seeing each other since last year. We've tried to keep it quiet, I didn't want to upset Dad. Now it's going to be impossible . . . because we've been doing more than seeing each other."

"All right."

She looked at him nervously, fearing his judgment. Her fingers dug into the sofa arm. "I'm pregnant, Rance."

He gazed impassively at her.

"You're not mad at me, are you?"

He hesitated, then said, "You know, I didn't have a very high opinion of Ricky Bible when he showed up on my doorstep to learn the ropes of the Christus. I found out, though, that he had been pigeonholed as a Christian teen idol much in the same way that I was typed as the Savior. I'm not saying that Ricky is a Renaissance man or anything, but there is a person there, a man of some character."

"That's what I've been trying to tell everyone," Evie muttered.

"Do you love him?"

"Yes."

"Then what's the problem? Are you worried what your dad is going to say?"

"No, not really. Well, maybe a little." She slumped down on the couch. "It's more where things are between me and Rick. And getting pregnant hasn't made things any easier. I look at him, think of him, differently now that he's doing the Savior roles. No offense, but he's becoming you. I'm in love with the Lord, and I'm carrying his baby. If I didn't already have a personal relationship with Jesus Christ, maybe things wouldn't be so tough."

"He's a man, Evie. A very mortal man. Just like me."

"But he's something more, too. Just like you. He's changing. He's closer to God than he was before. That's a good thing, isn't it?"

"A very good thing."

"Even if it drives us apart?"

"It's not an easy situation," said Rance.

"How did you handle it?" Evie asked. "You were married for a long time, before and after you became the Christus. Ten years?"

"Eleven, actually. Although Margorama and I were living apart the final year."

"How did you guys meet?"

"In a Bible-study class at church." His eyes shone with the memory. "I loved her spiritually the first time I set eyes on her."

"So everything was fine, at first."

"Oh, yes. It was wonderful. She was even thrilled when I got the role for *Hear the Word!* We were young and in love and with the Lord. We didn't know. Even after the first few films, I thought things were fine, but looking back I can see that there was a gap beginning to form. A distance."

"I can feel that already," said Evie.

"We weren't fighting or anything. It was more the way she looked at me, talked to me. There was a sense of reverence, perhaps even a little awe, that wasn't there before. It was a quiet change, and not at all negative. Who doesn't want to be revered? Still, it was just as destructive to our relationship as if we had been going at each other with kitchen knives."

"But it did get negative, didn't it?"

"Yes, and it began with the public appearances. I was away from home more, and it gave her time on her own, time to think. She may have resented my being gone more than the fact that I was playing the Savior. She may have been mad at the Lord for taking me away from her. In any event, we began to fight. She'd accuse me of having a holier-than-thou attitude, acting like I was better than her. Maybe it was true. Maybe I was all full of myself. Maybe I had a bit of a Messiah complex. Who was more qualified to have one?"

"There wasn't any way to rescue things once they got bad?"

Now Rance was on his feet, pacing. "We tried, we really did. We prayed, we sought the counsel of a minister, I even asked Noah for advice."

"What did he tell you?"

He hesitated. "Your father is a good man, Evie. I can say that now even after all that's happened. But I shouldn't have asked him to take sides on something that affected his business so directly."

"He wanted you to leave her."

Rance didn't respond. He was standing at the picture window, the midmorning sun at his feet, the shadows of leaves from the elm tree in the front yard rippling across the blue carpet.

"I'm sorry, Rance."

He stood silently for another moment, then turned back to her. "I'm not the only one," he said. "There were and are other Christi out there, in Passion Plays and church-produced theater productions and even on the roadside, carrying crosses on their stooped backs. There are Christi all over the place if people would just stop for a moment and take a look. And most of them have paid the price and will die in obscurity. Isn't that ironic? We cherish actors who play hoodlums, but ignore those who portray the most beloved figure in human history."

"I didn't realize there were so many others . . . I thought I was the only one. . . ."

He walked over to her. "It's a long casualty list, Evie. I know some of the men, and their families. Wally Emanuel, who did the Passion Play in Dillon, Montana, for many years. May through September, seven days a week, two shows a days. Married three times. Lives in a trailer. Hasn't seen his kids in a couple of years. Spends his days whittling sticks. He has terrible coughing fits and he's addicted to painkillers. He has to retire this year, and he doesn't have a pension. I visited him over the summer and took some guns out of his trailer."

"But what about his wives?"

"Penny was a dear. It was the first marriage for both of them. There was a problem with groupies in his younger years, Christ followers. She got tired of chasing them out of her front yard, taking the strange phone calls. Can you blame her? All she wanted was a normal life, which isn't easy in the Christus business. Especially in a small town."

"It must have been horrible."

"It's a rare individual who can stand up to those kind of rigors without cracking. You know, there used to be a sort of informal correspondence network among the women who were hooked up with the various Christi."

Evie got excited. "Really?"

"Of course, that was a long time ago, and I haven't been in touch with anyone besides Wally since I retired. But I can do some checking around and see what I can find."

"Gosh, Rance, I'd really appreciate it."

Unfortunately, Rance was unable to turn up anyone from his old circle of colleagues who still maintained a relationship with a Christus. They had all learned better, and were resolute about not returning to a life of glory and heartache. When Rance called with the bad news, Evie was disappointed but not dissuaded.

She placed a classified ad in *Women in Christ* magazine, as well as *Religious Entertainer Quarterly*. It read:

WOMEN OF CHRISTUS—YOU'RE NOT ALONE!
Support group forming for women in relationships with men who portray Jesus Christ. Share experiences, find a friend who understands. All welcome.

Evie sat back and waited for the responses to start overflowing her post-office box. Two weeks after her ad appeared, she found a single letter in the box. Its return address was Rancho Cucamonga, California. At last, Evie thought, ripping open the envelope right there in the post office.

It was a short letter. It said:

I always thought I would have to bear this alone. Please contact me immediately. I need your help.

Sincerely,

Tawny Grossheart.

Evie called the first member of her support group as soon as she got back to the office, shutting the door to ensure her privacy.

The voice that answered the phone sounded friendly and supportive enough.

"Tawny Grossheart?"

"Speaking."

"This is Evie Speck, from the Christus support group. We received your letter."

"Oh, wonderful! Thank you for calling."

"Our pleasure." Evie felt giddy. She had found a friend, someone who understood. "Are you married? Tell me about your husband. No, I'll tell you about my boyfriend first. He plays Jesus in the movies. It's hard to live with sometimes, since I already have a Savior, but I'm doing my best. You wouldn't believe all the weirdos I have to deal with. He says there's nothing to worry about, but I worry so much sometimes. Oh, I'm talking too much about myself. I want to know about you and your life. Are you married?"

"No, but I live with my boyfriend. He's on the stage."

"Yes, yes."

"He's starring in a play about the life of Muhammad."

There was silence on the line between Coon Rapids and Rancho Cucamonga.

"Hello?" inquired Cucamonga. "Are you still there?"

"Yes, I'm . . . I'm here," said Evie, confused. "Excuse me, but didn't the ad specify women who are involved with men who portray Jesus Christ?"

"Yes, but I didn't have anywhere else to turn. He's driving me crazy. Mecca this, Mecca that, and if you think you have problems with Christ fanatics, well, you haven't seen . . . "

Evie made a noise, unintelligible, sob-laden. She felt utterly disheartened.

"Please don't hang up," said the woman of Muhammad, her voice calm and soothing. "Are our situations so different that we can't find some common ground? I don't think we're so different. I bet we have a lot in common. Do you call your man Jesus by mistake sometimes?"

"I've done that," Evie said softly.

"I call mine Muhammad once in a while. And he calls me Aishah. We laugh about it, but it scares me, too."

"Yes. It creates a distance."

"Are you always worried about saying the right thing to him?"

"Always." Evie swallowed and wiped her eyes. "Look, I'm sorry I was cross with you. I was so excited to get your letter. It's the very first one I've gotten. You just caught me off guard."

"It's okay. I should have been clearer in my letter."

"But you're right," said Evie. "I think we probably do have a lot in common. I think we could help each other."

"I think so, too."

"Then it's settled. We're officially a support group. Women of Men Who Portray Christ or Any Other Deity."

"Thank you for being so broad-minded," Tawny said.

Twenty-Five

LEVITICUS' PRAYERS WEREN'T ANSWERED. NOT THE FIRST TIME HE FELT that his appeals had bounced off the bedroom walls and drifted up into the void. Over the years he had grown to trust and respect the whims of God's will, even if he didn't always understand it.

Leviticus felt a profound sense of guilt about the lies he had told. When *The Fetal Detective* had first entered his consciousness, his reaction had been one of animal panic. He had been running on instinct. But now that his lies of the moment had been transformed into a full-blown scheme, the shame of his deceit began to weigh on him.

A scheme. That's what Leviticus' noble intentions had resulted in. A fifth-rate, B-movie scheme. He felt foolish when he checked Nick and Rance into the hotel in Lynchburg. He felt ridiculous when he told Nick the crew was working around town shooting establishing shots for *FD*, when they were far away in Holy Land.

I'm no good at this, he told himself. I'm not a salesman. I don't like to manipulate people. And it's wrong to lie.

Yes, it was wrong to lie, but he was in too deep not to, and his prayers had not been answered.

On the second night, Leviticus stopped at the Lynchburg Lodge, room 1032. A disheveled and unshaven Nick Puckett opened the door, looking like he had skipped a trip or two to dreamland.

Rance was sitting slumped at a table, beer bottles at hand. A laptop computer and printer were on the bed. The kid handed Leviticus a thick stack of pages.

"New version," said Nick. "I changed some things. Hope you like it."

"I'll take a look right now." Leviticus came into the room and seated himself with great formality at the desk. He began to pretend reading, quickly, making sure to offer a selection of facial reactions.

Finally, Nick said, "I'm going to take a shower," and headed for the bathroom. When he heard the rush of water, Leviticus flipped the script upside down and checked on Rance. He had seen him in worse shape. Two beers wouldn't be enough to knock him out. They had probably worked straight through since check-in. Leviticus didn't disturb him.

After a few minutes the water shut off and Leviticus hustled back to the desk.

"Finished already?" Nick asked, vigorously rubbing his hair with a towel.

"You learn to read fast in this business," said Leviticus. "And no matter how fast someone reads this rewrite, they would have to be very impressed. Great job, Nick."

"Thanks!" said the kid, beaming.

"However," Leviticus said, turning the manuscript right side up, "there are a few spots that could use a little tweaking. . . ."

Nick nodded attentively. He didn't look disheartened at all. He looked ready to do whatever it took to make *The Fetal Detective* the best it could possibly be. Which disheartened Leviticus.

"There was something I was wondering about," Nick said, towel draped over his head.

"Okay."

"Well, I was wondering how you're planning to handle the special effects."

"The special effects . . ."

"You know, for the Fetal Detective. Rance is doing the voice, but how are you going to handle the fetus? Stop-motion animation? A puppet? A midget in a fetus suit?"

"Our special effects department is in charge of that," Leviticus said smoothly. "They do a bang-up job. Did you ever see *The Big Boat?*"

"Don't think so."

"Well, they created the illusion of The Great Flood, Noah's boat, the animals going two by two, the whole deal. It was spectacular. So one little fetus will be no sweat. I think you'll be pleasantly surprised at what they cook up."

This pattern continued all week. Days in Holy Land, evenings with the boys in Lynchburg, plotting nothing, telling lies, always telling lies. When Leviticus returned to his room, he hit the mattress without saying his prayers. What could he say? He couldn't face God now.

However, things were swell in Holy Land. Some fine barnyard vignettes for *Picture Window to Heaven.* The crew went about their business in a routine fashion. Leviticus' directorial style consisted of saying things like, "Let's get a shot of that," and "Hold on a minute, here comes a bus." At the end of the week they had accumulated miles of footage and were more than ready to pack up and return to beloved Coon Rapids.

"Say fellas, I'd like to make one more pass tomorrow morning before we leave," Leviticus announced as they loaded the equipment into the rental van. "I overheard someone say there was a neat depiction of Sodom and Gomorrah out behind the granary."

The crew groaned collectively.

"Come on, Leviticus," said Joe Gideon, longtime Good Samaritan cameraman. "We've already ruined enough film to make this movie and five sequels. Elijah won't use more than ten minutes of it."

"Well, I don't see how one more morning would hurt anything."

"I didn't even think we'd be here all week," said Joe. "Did Noah give us a real budget this time or something?"

"I got a good deal on the motel," Leviticus said.

"What a dump," someone inside the car muttered.

"It's not so bad," said Leviticus. "Our Savior often slept outdoors, on the bare ground."

"Ain't much progress for two thousand years."

"One more morning won't kill us," Leviticus told the heckler.

"One more morning and we'll start killing each other," Joe said. He immediately realized the error of his ways, and added, "Sorry, everyone. Do you guys forgive me?"

"Yah, yah, yah."

The mutiny continued once they got back to the cottages, but a promise of overtime pay prevailed where Christian principles had not. Once they were settled in for the night, Leviticus drove back to Lynchburg. This time, a fatigued Rance Jericho opened the door. Beyond him Leviticus could see Nick, sprawled on the bed, snoring lightly.

"He finally conked out an hour ago," whispered Rance. "I think he's been up for about four days straight."

"How about a nightcap?" Leviticus asked him. "You look like you could use it."

"You're an angel from God," Rance said.

They went down to the bar and found a corner booth. Leviticus ordered iced tea, Rance requested straight orange juice.

"Are you feeling okay, Rance?"

"I've got to cut back," he said. "My gut's been hurting lately."

"Mine too," said Leviticus. He leaned forward, arms resting on the table. "I guess things have gone pretty well," he said without enthusiasm.

"And once we get back home, then what?"

Leviticus shook his head. "I'm not sure. I don't suppose you'd be willing to put him up for a few days. He really likes you, Rance."

"I don't know. . . . "

"Look, if it's a matter of money . . ."

"No, it's not the money," said Rance. "I just don't want to hurt the boy. I've taken it this far, I did what you asked, and if you don't mind I'd like to ease my way out."

Nodding, Leviticus said, "I understand."

The drinks came, and they sat in silence, not looking at one another.

Finally, Rance said, "So what are you going to do with him?"

Leviticus sipped his tea. "I might take a gamble and send him home. Tell him my bosses decided the film wouldn't be commercial enough. Maybe he'll meet a nice girl and start a family and forget all about *The Fetal Detective*."

"He's been up for four days straight, Leviticus."

Leviticus laughed weakly. "Then I'm open to suggestions."

"Make the film."

"I've thought about it. I've prayed about it. But how would you shoehorn a message of love and compassion into a work like that? What would a Good Samaritan do if the Fetal Detective came his way?"

"Probably get caught in the crossfire."

"It's not that I think Nick is a bad person or anything," said Leviticus, "but he's only interested in the idea. That's what charges him, that's what keeps him going for four days without sleep, regardless of the moral implications of what he's creating."

"That's very true."

"I can't change his mind or his heart," said Leviticus, "because his feelings about the subject matter are so vague. He doesn't *care* about the abortion issue, he's just using it to fuel his imagination. . . . "

As I suspected all along, the dame who lived around me was in cahoots with the doctors.

I could hear them cutting their way through the abdomen, and then the uterus, and suddenly everything got real quiet. They knew I was waiting for them. I could sense it. And I didn't have to sprain my cerebellum to figure out who tipped them off.

I had relied on the dame for a lot these past nine months, but now I'd have to go it alone.

The next move was mine. . . .

Twenty-Six

THE FETAL DETECTIVE WAS FIRING THE IMAGINATION OF RANCE JERI-
cho, too. He loved playing a detective, even if it was just a preborn
one. Way back in his youth in McCorkle, North Dakota, he had
spent endless Saturday afternoons at the Princess Theater, watching, fascinated, the exploits of Sam Spade. He dedicated one whole
summer to talking tough and getting into trouble, until his father
gave him a whupping. Rance had toed the straight and true ever
since, and it was odd how now, as his career was dwindling and
burning away, this strange creation should be dropped into his life.

After Leviticus departed, Rance went out onto the balcony and
gazed at the lights of Lynchburg. He had enjoyed his week working with Nick more than any he could remember. The kid could really write dialogue. *Maybe I was in Christian cinema too long,*
Rance thought. *Maybe I don't know quality when I hear it. Maybe
it's just the lack of high-mindedness and pomposity that I find re-
freshing. The raw emotion, the frankness, the independence, the
life. Where every problem can be solved with a couple of slugs.
Where women can't be trusted. Where the battles aren't for your
eternal soul, just for the right to go on breathing another day.*

Rance felt something warm, deep down. The flame of his
dreams. It wasn't bright, but it still burned. He wanted to act. Not
for the money or the fame. For something else. For the love of the

craft, the creation of a character, making an audience believe in your portrayal.

I am an actor, he told himself, and I want to work.

Rance let Nick snooze all night, then around dawn slammed the bathroom door.

"Mrffggh," said the lump under the covers.

"Are you going to sleep all day?"

The sheet crept down, revealing a pair of tired eyes.

"We need to have a talk," said Rance.

Sitting up slowly, Nick said, "How long have I been out?"

"All night. Take a shower, and I'll get us some breakfast."

Nick did as instructed, while Rance ordered room service. After the food arrived, they sat on the beds and ate.

"What did you want to talk about?" Nick asked, spreading grape jelly on a slice of toast. "The script? I'll keep rewriting it for as long as it takes. I'll go without sleep for forty days and forty nights. I want it to be perfect."

"I know you do," said Rance. "I know you do." He found his appetite waning. "Now Leviticus, Leviticus, I've known that boy for a long time, ever since he was a kid. He's a good person, a fine Christian, and I've been blessed to have known him. Real blessed."

"He's a pretty cool guy."

"But he's under a lot of pressure, you understand. It's a tough business, this inspirational film business. You're not supposed to focus on the money; it's God's work and it's in God's hands, all those glorious sentiments meant for public consumption. If you want to survive, you've got to behave like any other business. Hold down expenses, be on the lookout for new trends, and keep tabs on what the competition is up to."

"That's what Mr. Countenance always tells me," said Nick. "He doesn't have any competitors yet, but he's worried that someone will move in on him. He says that the Christian bus drivers across America are his flock of lambs."

"Yes, and sometimes the pressures of business can lead people astray, make them do things that they wouldn't do under normal circumstances. They may be good and God-fearing on the inside, but sometimes these outside forces can be too much to handle."

"Yeah."

"I have something to tell you," Rance said, setting down his fork. "You're not going to like it."

"Well, okay. What is it?"

Rance looked carefully at Nick. "Kid, Good Samaritan has no plans to make *The Fetal Detective.*"

Nick smiled. "What's the punch line?"

"You're the punch line. Leviticus is a good person, but he's been leading you on. He's afraid of *The Fetal Detective* and what it might mean to Good Samaritan if it falls into the wrong hands. He wants to bury it."

The smile faded.

"It's a business deal, kid. Good Samaritan hasn't been faring too well lately, and there's a new player in Christian cinema, Blood of the Lamb Pictures. They make antiabortion shock films. They got a lot of attention at the Ark Awards, although they didn't win anything. They're ambitious and ruthless, according to Leviticus. He's afraid that if Blood of the Lamb got the rights to *The Fetal Detective,* they'd go from a minor player to an unstoppable force. I think his fears are exaggerated, but that's how he feels."

Nick abruptly got up and began pacing, shaking his head. "I knew it was too good to be true," he said. "I knew it."

"I'm sorry, son."

Nick turned to him. "You were in on it, then."

"Yes."

"Why are you telling me the truth now?" His eyes were hurt and narrow and wet.

"Because telling lies is a sin."

Silence, then: "How much did he pay you?"

"Nothing," Rance said. "I did it as a favor to him. He's my friend."

"And he doesn't know you've told me this?"

Rance shook his head.

"So you're betraying him."

"Better than betraying the Lord."

"You were betraying yourself."

"Not anymore. Rance Jericho is *not* the Lord."

"He's a saint, then."

"A man," said Rance. "A very flawed man. Now I know in my heart that I'm not closer to Him than anyone else. Quite honestly, I feel like shit."

"You're a sinner."

"Yes. And as a sinner, you'll have to forgive me if my motives in this matter are not entirely pure."

"Okay."

"I have a plan."

"Okay."

Rance moved to the window. Downtown Lynchburg lay at his feet. He didn't want dominion over all the world or even Lynchburg, just a tiny part of it. Was that so much to ask out of life?

"What do you see?" asked Nick.

Turning to him, Rance said, "A big city, with a lot of doctors."

Nick smiled, and added, "There was work to be done."

Rance came over to his protégé and embraced him. "Son," he whispered, "Rance Jericho *is* the Fetal Detective."

Twenty-Seven

AFTER A SLEEPLESS NIGHT TORN BY ANXIOUS CONTEMPLATION AND
desperate prayer, Leviticus decided sometime near dawn to reveal
all to Nicholas Puckett. He would go to his room, explain the situation, apologize, and ask for forgiveness. Then the burden would
be gone, and his conscience could rest.

It was the right thing to do, the Good Samaritan way.

The crew was scheduled to fly out of Lynchburg at noon,
Rance and Nick at two. Leviticus roused the crew early, grumbling
but happy to be pocketing the extra cash. He left them at Holy
Land, saying he was going to Lynchburg to look up an old nonex-
istent pastor friend. Leviticus went to the hotel, rode the elevator
to the tenth floor, and walked down the hallway to the room, all
the while rehearsing in his head what he must say. He prayed that
the news wouldn't crush the young man.

Arriving at room 1032, Leviticus knocked, waited, knocked
again. He called out their names. Perhaps they had fallen into an
exhausted sleep. He found a house phone and called the room.
There was no answer.

Maybe they went to breakfast, Leviticus thought, heading back
downstairs. He checked the café, no luck.

Finally, Leviticus approached the front desk.

"A couple of my friends are staying here," said Leviticus. "Room ten thirty-two. I registered for them earlier this week. My name's Leviticus Speck."

The clerk peered at a computer. "Room ten thirty-two, you said?"

"That's right."

"They checked out earlier this morning."

Leviticus stared blankly at him.

"Is there anything else I can help you with, sir?"

"Are you sure they checked out? They weren't supposed to be leaving yet."

"An older gentleman, longish hair, very distinguished-looking, and a younger man with dark hair, correct?"

"That's them."

"They checked out around eight."

"Did they say where they were going?"

"No, sir, although the older one did ask me where he could rent a car."

Leviticus wandered away from the desk, his lies spinning away, their razor knots disentangling from his heart. He sat down in a soft green chair not far away. They had gone. Rance had told him. It was over. Where had they fled to? The possibilities preyed on his mind, but at this moment Leviticus chose to focus on the positive, to celebrate the end of the lies.

However, a spiritual question remained unresolved. Leviticus had returned to the hotel with good intentions, planning to bare his soul to the kid. Were good intentions enough? Or did he actually have to speak the words, see them witnessed, and receive forgiveness?

Leviticus was uncertain on this matter, but knew he was eternally grateful that his prayer had been answered. Right there in the lobby at the Lynchburg Lodge he dropped to his knees and gave thanks to the Lord for delivering him from the madness of his lies and deceit. He again asked for forgiveness, and felt a blessing alight upon his heart.

On the flight home, Leviticus' soul brightened as the familiar tapestry of farmland and lakes passed beneath them. Life would return to normal as soon as the plane touched the ground. He could go back to thinking normal thoughts and reading normal scripts. When he saw Rick Bible, he would bear hug him and welcome him into the family. Forget the Arks, forget Channel Fifty-six, forget everything except the Word of God as revealed by the Holy Bible, King James Version or perhaps even the Revised Standard Version. Let them laugh in Tarzana. The Good Samaritan Way was the only way.

Still, on the walk through the vast reaches of the airport terminal, and on the short dark stroll across the farmyard to the Speck house, Leviticus felt a nagging sense of foreboding. He kept looking over his shoulder, thinking he was being followed, and seeing nothing, knowing someone was there, not a solicitor or a mugger but a fetus with an attitude.

Bad Samaritans

Twenty-Eight

A TRIO OF FLAGS FLAPPED CRISPLY ON POLES OUTSIDE THE CORPORATE headquarters of Blood of the Lamb International, Inc., located in an office park on the outskirts of Nashville. A corporate trinity. One was definitely the flag of the United States of America. The second seemed to be an unoccupied crucifix. The third held the visage of a lamb, a lamb in a bad mood, or so it appeared to Rance Jericho. What did that signify? he wondered, maneuvering the rental car into a visitors' parking spot. Next to them was a green hatchback sporting a bumper sticker: VISUALIZE UNBORN BABIES.

"I'm kinda scared," said Nick, staring at the low golden glass building. "What if this is another dead end? What if they don't take me seriously?"

"Don't worry, kid," Rance said. "They loved the script. And besides, they wouldn't set up a meeting for us with the president of the company if they didn't take you seriously."

"I hope you're right, Rance."

"I've got a good feeling about this." And he did. He had even sheared his legendary locks for the occasion. His scalp felt naked, his mind clear.

The pair left the car and proceeded to the main entrance. Another angry lamb shimmered in the reflective glass door, and it was no Virgin Mary illusion. Blood of the Lamb. Rance recalled what a shopper told him once, in those pathetic days when he haunted local Piggly Wigglys. *Born again with the blood of the lamb.* Rance thought he had a pretty fair understanding of Christianity—he wasn't the Savior, but he played Him in the movies—but this concept eluded him. He understood what born again meant, the almost mystical way the Savior could enter people's lives and renew their spirits. And he understood that the blood of the lamb was a metaphor for Christ, the Lamb of God, dying on the cross, shedding his blood so that the rest of humanity could avoid the eternity of emptiness that was hell.

But the linking of these tenets produced something strange, sinister. An image of violence, not love. An image of an angry lamb, bent on revenge.

"Good morning," said Rance, approaching the receptionist, a blond woman wearing a pretty blue dress with lace and beads. She looked friendly enough.

"Welcome to Blood of the Lamb. My name's Grace. How can I help you today?"

"We have an appointment with Mr. Paul Pedphill."

"And your names are?"

"I'm Rance Jericho. This is Nicholas Puckett."

She ran her finger down a list, then looked up and smiled. "If you'll have a seat, I'll let Mr. Pedphill know you're here."

"Thank you."

Rance's initial trepidation dissipated somewhat. This wasn't a cell of kooks. It was a real business, very professional, just like any other successful company. Only instead of lawn mowers, they sold antiabortion shock films.

In a short time a young man, clean-cut, in a dark suit, came into the reception area. "Mr. Jericho and Mr. Puckett?"

"That's us," Rance said, standing up.

"I'm Tad Lot, Mr. Pedphill's administrative assistant. Won't you follow me?"

They trailed the assistant through a maze of gray cubicles. "Nice weather we're having, isn't it?" said Tad.

"It's been very pleasant," Rance agreed.

"We could use some rain, though," Tad added. "The farmers really need it."

They headed down a narrow hallway which opened onto another reception area, fronting an office with a plaque on the door reading P. PEDPHILL, PRESIDENT, BLOOD OF THE LAMB PICTURES. Tad led them to the door, gave them a cheerful smile, and said, "Go right in. Mr. Pedphill is waiting for you."

"Thanks," Rance said. He gave Nick a pat on the shoulder. The kid was looking tense. "Let's do it, pal."

Nick nodded, and they went inside.

Pedphill's office was plain and unpretentious, with a bronzed fetus on a file cabinet and a map of the United States on the wall. What caught Rance's eye, though, was the array of miniature picture frames. They filled more than half the desk surface. All Rance could see were the backs of the frames from where he sat. The man who saw them all was slight, pale, and had the thinnest lips Rance had ever encountered. His handshake, though, was strong and aggressive.

"Gentlemen, please have a seat. It's a pleasure to meet both of you. Mr. Jericho, I've been an admirer of yours for some time. You're a credit to the industry. It's a shame your talents haven't been better utilized in recent years."

"Thank you," Rance said.

Pedphill turned his attention to Nick. "And your colleague here, Nicholas." He smiled, revealing baby teeth. "You understand, this isn't the normal treatment for writers who submit scripts to us." He picked up his copy of *The Fetal Detective* and stroked it. "But this, this is something else, something very special. God was looking over your shoulder when you wrote it. It's truly inspired."

"Thanks," Nick said.

Rance carefully watched his young author. He had coached Nick to let their hosts do all the talking. Be agreeable. And for God's sake don't tell them you haven't really thought much about the abortion issue.

"Where did you get the idea?" Pedphill asked.

"From a billboard." Nick sat forward, finally in comfortable territory. "A billboard with a golden fetus. I drive by it every day on the way to work." Nick told him about the whole vision thing.

"Fascinating," said Pedphill. "You must have very strong beliefs about our preborns."

Rance shut his eyes.

"Oh, sure," said Nick. "Fetuses are definitely getting the short end of the stick."

Rance breathed again.

"Exactly," said Pedphill. "Why, do you know that a fetus has never had a starring role in a major motion picture? Or even a supporting role? Is it just coincidence? We don't think so. Hollywood is biased against preborns. That's why your script is so ground breaking. We've made plenty of films where the fetus is the victim, but never one where the fetus is the hero."

Nick nodded.

"I don't know how familiar you are with our films," Pedphill continued, "but frankly we've been struggling. I'm not happy with the scripts we've been getting lately. We're in something of a rut. If we don't take the next step, the films will become a joke, a sideshow, and we won't be taken seriously. We're not about profits or awards. There are millions of innocent lives on the line. Blood of the Lamb will not let them down. With God's help, we won't." He paused, and laid his hands on the manuscript. "With *The Fetal Detective*, we won't."

"With God's help," Rance echoed.

"So what are you doing now?" Pedphill asked Nick. "For employment, I mean."

"I'm an editorial assistant at *Christian Bus Driver* magazine."

"How would you like to work in the movie business?" Pedphill asked quietly, without a smile.

"I'd like that more than anything, sir." Nick glanced at Rance. "But it has to be with the understanding, Mr. Pedphill, that Rance is part of the deal. He has to be the Fetal Detective. We've worked on the script together, he's perfect for the role."

"Kid, don't put Mr. Pedphill in that position," Rance said. This scene they had not rehearsed. Nick was improvising, rushing things. Now wasn't the time to be making demands.

"Well, that's how I feel about it," said Nick. "I can't help it."

Paul Pedphill laughed. "I'm sure we can work something out," he said. "It would be quite a change, having a professional actor in one of our films." He gestured, writing a phantom marquee. *The Fetal Detective*, Starring Rance Jericho." He stood up. "But that's down the long road ahead of us. Why don't I show you around the place, introduce you to a few people?"

They left the office and headed back into the land of cubicles. "This room," Pedphill said, "is the finance area for the entire corporation. We're involved in numerous ventures, from gospel music to garbage hauling. We call and do mailings to our Blood of the Lamb family, asking support for our upcoming projects. This is how *The Fetal Detective* will get financed, too. As I'm sure you know, Rance, the Christian film business isn't as lucrative as its secular counterpart, so we have to be creative. Later this year we'll be staging a telethon in conjunction with *Blood of the Lamb Theater*. Hopefully, as the movie division grows and we win a wider audience, the films will turn a profit and we'll be less dependent on solicitation and the good graces of our corporate elders and then we will be able to really pump some money into the production end."

"Interesting," said Rance.

"Oh, here's someone I'd like you to meet," Pedphill said, stopping at a corner cubicle. There was a woman inside, middle-aged, wearing a veiled black dress. Her desk was overwhelmed with tiny gold frames, too. But this time Rance could see the photographs.

"This is Betty Excelsior, who is in charge of our direct-mailing operation. Betty, this is Nicholas Puckett, a new screenwriter, and Rance Jericho, who's joining us as an actor."

"A blessing to meet you," Betty said, lifting her veil.

"Hi," said Nick, shaking her hand.

Rance said hello and clasped her hand, too, but his eyes were focused elsewhere.

"Doesn't Betty have a lovely family?" Pedphill said.

"Very lovely," Rance replied vaguely. As she talked about her job and all the exciting things happening at Blood of the Lamb, Rance kept staring at the pictures. He was confused inside. Betty did keep what society commonly thought of as family photos on her desk. A freckled boy, perhaps ten, wearing a red cowboy hat. A pair of teenaged girls. A balding, kind-faced husband.

But that was only a fraction of the Excelsior clan. There were humans in all stages of development, from the nearly viable to mere specks in a murky sea. No doubt these were photos of her grown children at various stages of their maturation. Unusual certainly, but nothing that peculiar. The President himself apparently had a similar display on his desk.

Was it a matter of some delicacy for her? Rance wasn't sure, so he waited until they were walking along again, and asked their host, "Those photos on her desk. . . ."

"She has one of our bigger families," Pedphill said. "Fifty-seven kids at last count. Not to brag, but I've got a hundred and five myself. Of course, these are all rough estimates. How many kids do you have?"

"I thought I had one. . . ."

"It's okay," said Pedphill. "Not everybody has caught on to our way of counting. You see, life begins at conception, so whether or not these babies make it out into the so-called real world isn't relevant. A human life is a human life. Many of my children have died accidentally. Most of the time it's not my wife's fault, it's just God's will that they didn't get a good grip on the wall of her uterus. But that doesn't make them any less important as people, although I must confess that once we hit fifty it became hard to remember all their names."

"I can imagine," said Rance.

"That's something we're going to have to discuss," Pedphill said to Nick. "The name of the film."

From the phone banks they proceeded to the production area, a series of small offices and soundstages, not so different at all from Good Samaritan.

Paul Pedphill stopped outside one of the offices and said, "I want you fellows to meet someone who you will be working with very closely over the next few months."

A bald man in a green turtleneck and gold-rimmed glasses, several days growth of graying beard on his tanned face, was on the phone. He gave a short wave and held up two fingers to Pedphill as they entered the room.

BOL movie posters blanketed the walls. Rance felt like he was under surveillance by dozens of pairs of unborn eyes.

They waited, Rance picking up snatches of the conversation, something about fetal continuity. The exchange became quite heated, then finally the man hung up and came around the desk.

"Any problems?" asked Pedphill.

"Nothing a little fake cord blood won't clear up," said the man, who glanced expectantly at the guests.

"Josh, this is Nick Puckett, Rance Jericho." As they exchanged handshakes, Pedphill said, "Guys, this is Joshua Crippen, the best director I've ever worked with. He never met a fetus he didn't like. You may be familiar with his résumé: *Prenatal Massacre, Doctor of Darkness, Womb of the Living Dead.* He's excited about *The Fetal Detective,* too, aren't you, Josh?"

"That's right," he said. "Great story, Nicholas. One of a kind. I hope we have an opportunity to work together and bring *The Fetal Detective* to life. I'm a very writer-friendly director."

Nick nodded, but didn't say anything.

"Where did you ever get an idea like that?" asked the director.

"From God," Nick said.

"I thought so." He turned to Rance. "I'm a fan of your work, too, sir."

"Thanks," said Rance.

"Mr. Jericho has a home here, if he wants it," said Pedphill.

"Yes," Nick said quickly, "he's going to be the Fetal Detective."

"I've never worked with a professional actor before," Crippen told him. "It'll be a treat."

"I wanted to ask you something," said Nick, addressing both of the Blood of the Lamb men.

"What is it, Nick?" Pedphill asked.

"Well, I was just wondering how you plan to do the special effects. It's got me a little worried. I know you don't have very big budgets."

"Ideally," said the director, "we would use an actual fetus, then just have Rance do the voice-over."

"We use one hundred percent genuine innocent unborn aborted babies in all our films," Pedphill added. "It's the trademark of Blood of the Lamb."

"But this is a special case," Crippen continued. "The script calls upon the preborn one to maneuver in an athletic style which may be beyond the capabilities of even the most viable fetus."

"That doesn't make the unborn baby any less important than you or I," Pedphill broke in. "We do recognize the limitations of the preborn. Who doesn't have limitations? We've all got limitations. I can't water ski, for instance. Neither can an unborn baby. I've never climbed a mountain, either. See, we're actually more alike than different when you sit down and actually study the situation."

"The point is," said Crippen, "we can't fall back on our standard routines for *The Fetal Detective*. We'll have to innovate, improvise. It'll be good for us, and it will be good for the film, too. The fetus effect is definitely the first problem we should address, though."

"I was thinking maybe a midget in a fetus suit," Nick said sincerely.

The director thought for a second, then said, "Well, we shouldn't shut the door on any idea at this point."

Back in his office after the tour ended, Paul Pedphill said, "As I mentioned before, we need to discuss the title."

"Don't you like it?" Nick asked.

"It's a snappy title, don't get me wrong. But the term *fetus* has such cold, clinical implications. It makes abortion seem almost palatable. As we all know, an individual in the womb is no different than you or I, they're just a bit smaller and not as well informed. We prefer the term *preborn*, although I admit that *The Preborn Detective* doesn't quite have the same ring to it as your title."

"Maybe the Fetal Detective is a nickname given to him by the bad guys," Rance suggested. "They use it to disparage him, like, 'Aw, he's not so tough, he's just a fetal detective.' Maybe he refers to himself as a P.I., Preborn Investigator." He looked at Nick, who seemed receptive.

"Yes, that has possibilities," Pedphill said, nodding. "We mustn't forget that there are certain sensitivities to consider in terms of our core audience. They may prejudge the film based on the title alone. Hopefully, we've built up a relationship of trust by now. We'll have to get the word out early and reassure them."

Rance liked what he was hearing from the head of Blood of the Lamb Pictures. Practical, calm, sensitive to the sensibilities of both the public and the artist.

Pedphill got a faraway look in his eyes. "We could use a series of billboards. Start simple: an unadorned preborn, A CHILD OR A CHOICE. Change the message every week—the number of abortions performed in the country annually, the grisly details of the procedure, lay it all out. Then add a few physical touches: the fedora, the gun, and a new message: STARTING TOMORROW, IT'S PAYBACK TIME." He looked at Rance and Nick. "What do you think?"

"You're really going to make my movie, aren't you?" Nick said with some emotion.

"Son, Blood of the Lamb is not just going to make *The Fetal Detective*," Paul Pedphill said quietly, leaning forward, "I intend for *The Fetal Detective* to make Blood of the Lamb."

Twenty-Nine

LIFE SHOULD HAVE GOTTEN ROSY AFTER LEVITICUS LAID HIS BURDEN down in Lynchburg. After all, he had placed the fate of *The Fetal Detective* in the Lord's hands, where it rightfully belonged. He just didn't feel comfortable passing judgment on such high matters, for fear of being judged himself. He felt humble and marginally holy. Perhaps the arrival of *The Fetal Detective* would make the world a better place in which to live. Miracles happen.

This whole episode had been a distraction, tearing him away from his relationship with the Lord and his one true mission: making wholesome, positive inspirational films. This calling was nothing to be ashamed of. Maybe Good Samaritan needed to refine its approach to the art of film, modernize things a bit, but that didn't mean their basic tenets were invalid.

Leviticus was even working up some enthusiasm for *Picture Window of God*. Dad had been well pleased with the footage Leviticus and the crew had brought back from the Dixie Holy Land. Elijah was knocking the script into shape, and the end result would be a solid, entertaining, uplifting motion picture.

Also, work on the second entry in the Savior Mach II series, *Heaven Needs You!*, was nearing completion. Evie had already set up promotional events at several area churches, the first in two weeks at the Speck's own house of worship, Christ the Reliever. Evie seemed happier and more on top of things lately, and Rick Bible in turn.

There were good signs all over, in and around the life of Leviticus Speck.

Then, three days and a morning after Leviticus returned from Virginia, he got a call from Bob Countenance at *Christian Bus Driver.*

"Leviticus, a blessing to talk with you," said the editor.

"A blessing to hear from you, Bob," Leviticus replied. "It's been a while."

"Too long. Say, I got an interesting phone call last night."

"You did?"

"It was from my former editorial assistant. Called to say he found a job with a motion-picture studio. I was darn surprised to hear it wasn't Good Samaritan."

Leviticus waited, his heart plunging at the realization that his lies still had life, could still hurt him. What had Nicholas told Bob?

"I . . . I guess I wasn't entirely surprised," Leviticus offered.

"Well, I appreciate the fact that you were honest with him. I know well enough what it's like to operate on a tight budget. I'm sorry you weren't able to work something out."

"Yes, well, it was unfortunate," Leviticus said. Am I lying again, he wondered, by not telling Bob the complete story? But this was Nick's choice. If, out of a sense of compassion and charity, the kid chose to protect Leviticus' reputation, then he should not shun this gift. Just call him and say God bless you. "Have you found a replacement for him?"

"Not yet. Rosemary is on a break from her studies, so she's coming in to help out, and hopefully I'll find a permanent replacement soon, maybe someone with not quite so much talent."

"God be with you on your search."

"Actually, Leviticus, that wasn't the main reason I called," said Countenance. "Forgive me for adding to your burden, but I've had to make some difficult decisions, too, about the magazine. The circulation has been stagnant the past few years, and I've been searching for ways to increase our readership, serve our readers better."

"Okay."

"I've decided to tighten the focus of the magazine, and eliminate those parts that aren't essential to the Christian bus driving community. Unfortunately, that means I'm dropping a number of the columns, including yours. I'm sorry, Leviticus. Don't feel bad, though. I also pulled the plug on 'Hobby Corner' and 'Where's Judas?' "

Even though Leviticus had occasionally entertained notions of quitting, getting the ax still stung. "Well, Bob, I understand your situation. It was a privilege to have been a contributor for so long."

"Hey, it was a blessing having you as a columnist, and I mean that sincerely. I always enjoyed reading it."

"Thanks."

"Tell your father I said hello, and good luck to you, Leviticus. Call me anytime. Stay in touch, okay?"

"I will do that. Have a blessed day, Bob."

"Right back at you, Leviticus."

Leviticus was philosophical about saying so long to the world of journalism. What had begun as an enjoyable diversion, and an opportunity to educate and enlighten, had become something of a chore over the past year. He never had much luck visualizing the audience for the magazine. Were Christian bus drivers really all that different from their secular brethren? Were there Christian and non-Christian ways to drive a bus? There probably were. Christian drivers obey the speed limit, shun tailgating, let their fellow drivers merge, and keep their use of the horn to a minimum, perhaps a gentle tap when the driver ahead doesn't notice that the light has changed to green. So a magazine for Christian drivers of all stripes, that would fill both a practical and spiritual need. The only difference between bus driving and regular driving, really, was that in the former situation one carried more passengers.

But that's Bob's business, Leviticus told himself. He's not asking for my help or advice. Take care of your own house, and leave the driving to the Lord.

The following week a bout of bronchitis got a grip on Leviticus. He had, as his grandmother used to say, the "croup." At the weekly Good Samaritan board meeting he mostly listened and took notes.

"Just keep your distance from Rick," Noah said. "We can't afford to have a hoarse Christus at the beginning of a promotional tour."

"I'm not contagious anymore," Leviticus bleated.

"You sound horrible," Evie told him.

"Thanks."

"Maybe you should go to the doctor," she said.

"It's not as bad as it sounds," said Leviticus, almost whispering.

"Let's all put in a word for Leviticus when we say our prayers tonight," Noah said, "but right now I'd like to get down to business. Evie, is everything set for next Tuesday?"

"Yes, we're ready," she said, looking at a legal pad. "Rick will be arriving at Christ the Reliever at 7 P.M. Pastor Diggs will give an approximately fifteen-minute sermon on the value of Christian popular art, Rick will perform an excerpt from the Sermon on the Mount, followed by a clip from *Heaven Needs You!*, after which there will be a question-and-answer session, with lemonade and cookies served by the Ladies' Auxiliary."

"Which clip are you planning to show?" Leviticus asked.

"The 'World Without Jesus' sequence," said Noah.

Leviticus nodded. "World Without Jesus" occurred midway through the film, when the Savior takes a single mom on a tour of a world in which He never existed. Lots of Buddhists and Muslims and so forth. And earthquakes and hurricanes. And pain. Of course, this was Good Samaritan, so the images were conjured up mostly via the dialogue route, along with a modicum of stock footage of natural disasters. Talk was cheap, and the imagination was the best special. . . .

"You know," his father said, "the imagination is the best special-effects factory ever invented."

"A good thing for us," said Leviticus.

Noah gave his son an unamused look and turned to Evie. "Has Rick been rehearsing his speech? How is it going?"

"He's been working on it all week," she said. "He knows it forward and backward. He'll do a great job."

"Try to stress the importance of projection when speaking in front of a live audience," her father said. "He tends to mumble sometimes, which you can get away with on film, but that won't cut it in public. And remind him to stay in character."

"Yes, Dad," she said tersely.

"Make sure he brings his Ark Award, too."

"Yes, Dad."

Noah looked at his son, then his daughter. "Any other business that needs addressing?"

"Well," said Leviticus, "Bob Countenance says hello."

"Good. How is he faring? How is his new assistant working out?"

"He worked out too well," said Leviticus. "Already found a better job."

"He sure didn't last long."

"Bob's also dropping my column."

"He's dropping *you*?"

"Yes."

"Why? You haven't been missing your deadlines, have you?"

"No, nothing like that. He just wants to take the magazine in a new direction. I wasn't the only one to get the bad news; he also terminated 'Hobby Corner'."

"Boy, there's going to be a lot of half-built Sistine Chapels out there," Noah said. "What are the readers supposed to do with all those leftover toothpicks?"

Leviticus shrugged. "Everything changes, Dad."

"The Gospel never changes."

Leviticus was going to contradict his father, inform him that sometimes change was necessary, that change didn't have to mean uprooting your basic principles, but he didn't. That disrespectful attitude was what got him into trouble in the first place.

"You're right," Leviticus rasped. "We should stay true to our beliefs, not twist in the wind. I'm just impatient. I want good things to happen to Good Samaritan. Now and forever."

That night, as he lay on his bed in the moonlight, trying to subdue a coughing fit, Leviticus folded his hands and made the connection.

Lord, what's happening to me? I'm ready to be normal again, I really am, but something is holding me back. Why do I keep seeing the possibilities? Why can't I be as satisfied and certain as my father? I never used to be this way. I used to be satisfied, as far back as I can remember. I was always filled up. But these days I'm hungry, and I don't know what will fill the hole.

Thirty

THAT NIGHT, EVIE CALLED THE WOMAN IN THE LIFE OF THE MAN WHO played Muhammad. The Man himself answered, which Evie hadn't expected.

"Hello?"

Evie quickly hung up, then punched the number again. "Uh, hi. Is Tawny there?"

"Yep, hang on."

A few moments later:

"Hello?"

"Tawny? Evie."

"Well, hi. I've been thinking of calling you. How have you been?"

"Okay, I guess. I got scared when he answered. That was him, wasn't it?"

"Yes, could you tell?"

"Absolutely. Isn't that funny? I felt the same way I do when Rick answers the phone. The same nervousness, the same impulse to avert everything in sight. And I don't even know anything about Muhammad. I don't even know what he looks like."

"You sound so troubled, Evie. What's going on?"

"Oh, my dad said something that upset me."

"About Rick?"

"Yes. He said I should make sure he stays in character during his personal appearances. I bit my tongue. But I was thinking, well, it won't be hard for him to stay in character, because every day I'm seeing less and less difference between them."

"You haven't told your father anything, then."

"No. I've been meaning to, we've been meaning to, but the time never seems to be right."

"Have you made a decision on your pregnancy yet?"

"No. It's really confusing. There are so many things to think about."

"Have you talked to anyone?"

"My brother and I talk. Or rather, I talk and he listens, wincing all the while."

"I mean a professional, someone who can tell you what challenges you'll be facing no matter what you decide."

"No, I haven't."

"Well, I think things would get easier on you, once you make the decision."

"Yeah. I suppose."

"What about you and Rick? How does he feel? Does he want the same things you do?"

"He's been really busy lately, so we haven't had much personal time. But he has been very supportive all along."

"So what are you afraid will happen if you tell your dad?"

"I don't know. If it were anybody else, this wouldn't be such an ordeal. But Rick, the whole future of the company depends on him. At least that's how Dad is acting. It's a whole image thing he's trying to cultivate. He's on some kind of purity kick with Rick. He'll think I'm completely selfish if he finds out. He'll guilt me from about nine different directions."

"I wonder if you and Rick would be doing better if the pressure from your father was taken away. It's hard enough trying to build a relationship for someone in your situation, without your parents interfering. How does your mom feel about it?"

"Don't know. She died when I was a kid."

"I'm sorry. I didn't realize."

"That's all right. Listen, I want to know how you're doing, Tawny. Is everything okay?"

Her voice dropped. "I can't really talk now, Evie. I haven't told him about you. Are you going to be around this weekend? Can I call you then?"

"Of course. That's what our support group is all about."

"Thank you. I'll talk to you later."

"Bye."

That evening, Evie visited her own deity and helped him rehearse the Sermon on the Mount. He was dressed in his full Christus regalia. A television played in the background, sound down. A videotape of *Hear the Word!*, in all its black-and-white glory. Just another normal Thursday night.

"The light of the body is the eye," he said. "If therefore thine eye be single, thy whole body shall be full of light. But if thine eye be evil, thy whole body shall be full of darkness. If therefore the light that is in thee be darkness, how great is that darkness!"

"That's good," Evie said. "Try to make your hand gestures a little more natural. They're distracting from your beautiful face."

The Christus blushed. "I'm trying to stay in character, Evie."

"Sorry. Just find that middle ground. It's not like film acting; you do have to worry about people in the back rows, but it's a small venue so you don't have to shout."

"Gotcha." He turned. "Be right back. Bathroom break."

While he was gone, Evie gazed languidly at the television. Rance looked so handsome in his younger days. She sighed, hugging a pillow. The screen flickered. Rance was speaking to a crowd on a dusty street. His eyes found the camera for a moment, and suddenly the volume shot up, and she heard him say, "Your friend is right, Evie. You shouldn't try to deceive your father, even in an innocent way, because in the end you'll only deceive yourself. Your secrets are burdens which are preventing you from enjoying your life and a full relationship with me. Give them up and be at peace, Evie. Give them up, give them up. . . . "

"How's the movie?"

Evie sat up abruptly. This year's Christus was standing before her, a piece of toilet paper stuck to his sandal. She glanced at him, then looked at the television screen. Rance was no longer giving her the eye. His lips were moving, his voice muted.

"I've seen this movie so many times," she said, "but it seems like every time I get something more out of it."

"Well, it is a classic."

Evie stood up and switched off the television, and what was left was a great darkness.

Thirty-One

"I DON'T KNOW IF I CAN GO THROUGH WITH THIS," SAID RICK BIBLE, outfitted in robe and sandals and parka, as they drove to his first personal appearance at Christ the Reliever Church.

"Nervous?" Leviticus asked. He looked over at the new Christus. Didn't appear nervous. Disheartened was more like it. "You've done enough of these to know the scene. It doesn't matter that it's our home church. Go in, say your piece, throw a little Ricky Bible charisma around, and then go home. Nothing to it."

"I know. I'm not really worried about it."

"Then what? Are you feeling sick?" Evie had caught whatever malady had knocked down Leviticus. She had been in bed since yesterday afternoon. His own voice still showed a strain, although it did seem to be improving.

"I think I should talk to Pastor Diggs before my appearance."

Leviticus glanced at him again, and checked his watch. Whatever spiritual crisis he was experiencing, he had better solve it fast. They were running late. The waiting congregation may not know the day or the hour when the Lord will come, but punctuality was expected of their Christi. Leviticus stepped hard on the accelerator.

It was five minutes before seven when they turned the familiar corner where the oak tree had been split in two by a lightning strike some years back, a warning to rowdy confirmation students.

The parking lot at Christ the Reliever was virtually empty. Leviticus wondered if they had come on the wrong night.

"I'm sure the place will fill up," said Leviticus. "It's still early."

Rick didn't seem to notice. He stared out the window, somber-faced.

A simple sign outside the brick building said:

**IN PERSON—RICK BIBLE AS THE SAVIOR—
HEAVEN NEEDS YOU!—TUES., 7 P.M.**

They parked by a snowbank at the back entrance. Leviticus grabbed the Ark Award, and they headed inside.

"Sorry there isn't more of a turnout," said Pastor Diggs, who was coming down the hallway when they entered the church offices. "We ran an announcement in the bulletin last Sunday, but many in our flock are snowbirds. They'll be in Arizona until April, I'm afraid."

"Maybe we should wait until quarter after or so," Leviticus suggested, tugging off his boots. "In case there are stragglers."

"Yes," said Rick, "I need to talk to you, Pastor Diggs."

The pastor surveyed Rick. "You certainly do bear an amazing resemblance to our Savior, even with the parka."

"Can we talk in your office?"

"Come this way."

"I'll wait in the library," said Leviticus, giving Rick a poke on the arm.

Leviticus had just settled into a deep, lumpy leather chair and was absorbed in the latest issue of *Christian Librarian* magazine ("Overdue Books: The Silent Sin") when a downcast Rick Bible appeared in the doorway.

"That was quick," Leviticus said. The wonderful thing about spiritual problems was that all the answers were contained in one book, and nobody knew that book better than Pastor Diggs.

Rick came in, dropped into a chair. "He didn't want to talk to me."

"Why?"

"He said he didn't feel comfortable offering spiritual advice to someone who so closely resembled his Savior. He wanted to ask me for advice on *his* problems."

Leviticus knelt down in front of Rick's chair. "What's going on? Maybe I can help."

Rick, his eyes pained, looked at Leviticus for a long time. "It's about me and Evie," he finally said. "No one knows this, but we're . . . we're a couple."

"I know."

Rick appeared surprised, less than omniscient. "When did you find out?"

"I've known for a long time. Don't worry, I haven't told anyone."

"Thanks, Leviticus. You're a good brother."

Leviticus stood up. "You know, I have to say that I didn't think much of Ricky Bible. Maybe I was envious, maybe I wasn't looking at you as a person, just the image. I don't know. But you're different now. Something's different about you. And I like it."

"That's the whole problem," said Rick. "Evie's treating me like a stranger. The way she looks at me sometimes, I don't think she even sees me. She acts like she's afraid of me."

"But your manner is so much more gentle and caring these days. What could she be afraid of?"

"I don't think she likes the changes. We talked about it the other night. It was really hard. She's worried that I'm becoming another Rance. I told her she was wrong, but now I'm beginning to wonder."

"Rance is a good man."

"But not every woman wants to date her personal Savior. I have changed, Leviticus, but I thought I was just maturing. Maybe I am becoming the role I'm playing. Maybe I am having trouble putting the robe and sandals away at the end of the day. Maybe that's what she's afraid of."

"Maybe."

"Look at me," Rick said, rising. He lifted his arms. "Most men my age are at home this time of night, remodeling their dens, or watching a ball game, or playing with their kids. Not me. I'm running around town in a Christ costume. For what? Why can't I have a normal life? Is that so much to ask?"

"It's a high calling," said Leviticus, wanting to settle down his star. "It's the greatest role ever for an actor. You can change lives with your art. That's nothing to be ashamed of."

Rick shook his head. "I never should have agreed to it. I should have seen this coming. It ruined Rance's life, and it's going to ruin mine, too."

"You could try some different roles. It's not too late. You're only on your second Savior film. Rance made eight or ten before he really became identified with the role."

"Noah will never allow it," said Rick. "He's grooming me. He sent me to study with Rance because he wants me to be Rance. He wants me to be typecast as the Savior. That would be a success for him."

"I can try talking to him," Leviticus offered.

"No, it won't work. Don't you remember the argument we had about the farmer role in *Picture Window of God?* Even if I raised the biggest hog in the state, he would have found some reason why I wasn't right for the part. No, Leviticus, this is something I have to solve on my own. I don't know how, but Evie's too important to me not to try."

Blessed are the pure in heart, Leviticus thought, for they shall see God.

Then he saw that it was 7:15. "Come on, buddy," Leviticus said, taking the Christus by the arm. "Time to be the Lord."

"I'm a sinner," Rick said, his white garment sweeping across the floor. "I'm really not a very good person."

"You're not so bad," Leviticus said. "In fact, I kinda like you."

The church was barely a quarter full. Rick did a good job with the Sermon on the Mount, and answered the questions deftly enough, although he fumbled for a moment when asked which actress he most enjoyed working with. But he came up with the perfect response: Lovey Molley, best known for her appearance as Mrs. Olson in *The Good Neighbor*, who was hot only in the spiritual sense. He got a nice round of smiles for that one. The clip ran without technical problems, too. All in all, a successful if not spectacular event. The sparse attendance was a concern, though.

There was no applause at the end, but then Leviticus wasn't expecting any.

Thirty-Two

BLOOD OF THE LAMB TREATED *THE FETAL DETECTIVE* LIKE A DOTING mother. Every need was tended to, every desire fulfilled. Nothing was too good for their golden boy; he got the best in preproduction care. The studio had high hopes for him. Paul Pedphill and company expected him to really make his mark on the world.

Even so, there were limitations to their love. The seed money was coming in at a steady, if not spectacular rate, which necessitated the usual modest budget and short production schedule. The invisible congregation was taking its time getting acquainted with the newcomer; some did not immediately grasp the concept. "Preborns can't carry much less use firearms," a Mrs. Ramjet wrote to Paul Pedphill after receiving a promotional flyer for the film. "It doesn't make any sense. How can he see where he's going? And where did he get the hat?"

BOL responded with patience and understanding toward those righteous lambs who lost their way in Nicholas Puckett's mind. In the case of Mrs. Ramjet, Paul Pedphill personally wrote her a reply:

Dear Mrs. Ramjet,

Thank you very much for your very thoughtful letter. I understand your confusion concerning our upcoming release, The Fetal Detective. *It is accurate that the vast majority of preborns could not use firearms and would most likely not wear a hat while in the womb. However, the Fetal Detective is a fictional character, much like the Lone Ranger or Robin Hood. He's a defender of justice. He stands up and fights for the rights of the preborn. He's a hero, the first hero of the pro-life movement. Please accept this autographed photograph of the Fetal Detective as a token of thanks for your interest in this exciting new project.*

God Bless You,

Paul Pedphill

President, Blood of the Lamb Pictures

Mrs. Ramjet's letter was not the only one of this ilk, so Pedphill and his staff decided to mount an educational campaign aimed at making the Fetal Detective accessible to all. The Fetal Detective couldn't take over the world unless he had a little help, so they made a to-do list. First and foremost on the list was the need to establish the name of the Fetal Detective.

This need was attacked on a number of fronts. Promotional packets were assembled and mailed to both Christian and secular media outlets. These packets included a one-page plot summary, a FAQ sheet which covered many of Mrs. Ramjet's concerns, a pro-life noir photo of Rance Jericho as the Fetal Detective, an FD bumper sticker, and for good measure a glossy color snapshot of an innocent unborn mutilated aborted baby.

Moreover, BOL gave *Christian Film Review* exclusive rights to the making of *The Fetal Detective* story. Paul provided *CFR* editor and publisher Buck Verily with unlimited access to the set and encouraged everyone working on the movie to give him their full cooperation. Strong early word on the film from a source as respected as *Christian Film Review* could multiply the number of initial orders received five or even tenfold. And it couldn't hurt come Ark Awards time.

BOL also donated the Fetal Detective's services to the Drug

Lords, a pro-life splinter group dedicated to combating the spread of antiabortion pills. Paul was sympathetic to their cause. Antiabortion drugs were the most insidious development in the baby-killing field since the invention of the coat hanger. It was so impersonal. You didn't have to confront the victim face-to-face.

Paul was tempted to suggest to Nick that he include a scene about baby-killing pills in his script, but decided against it, thinking that the action sequences would suffer. Lack of an easily identified villain; although doctors did prescribe the drug, they did not administer it.

The Fetal Detective did donate his time for a thirty-second public-service announcement that ran on the Resurrection Broadcast Network and other religious empires near the top of the dial:

"There's a new weapon in the war against unborn babies. It's no bigger than a slug from a thirty-eight. It's a poison pill. RU-666, I like to call it. As we all know, surgical abortions can't be performed on babies younger than six weeks. It's no mystery that this deadly weapon was designed to target the most vulnerable of the unborn, those barely formed and a long way from viability. Stop this chemical assassination of innocent people. I'm doing my part. Why don't you do yours and call the number on your screen now?"

BOL also licensed the Fetal Detective to Holy Ink Press, a Christian comic-book company based in Wichita, which immediately began production on the first in a series of graphic novels based on the adventures of the Unborn Avenger. The comics were to be distributed to Sunday schools and confirmation classes. Paul had struggled over the decision whether to require the artists and writers to sanitize the content for the younger audience. Not an easy call. What if the children who picked up a Fetal Detective comic had parents who had not yet shared the basics of human reproduction with them? It would be a rather abrupt introduction to the miracle of life. Paul did not wish to usurp parental authority. On the other hand, the sooner children knew that their little brothers and sisters were getting their heads punctured and brains sucked out the better.

However, the most ambitious idea in the early promotional efforts for the Fetal Detective was Project Billboard. Paul's appointed designates met with leaders of right-to-life groups across the country in order to work out a cooperative agreement for use of the billboards as the release date of the film neared. The percentage of the rental fee paid by BOL would increase as their message gradually dominated the billboards. Some of the groups were willing to donate the space, if given a mention in the closing credits. Many of these billboards were fixtures in their communities, the golden unborn babies familiar faces that motorists felt like they knew on a first-name basis. So it would be very effective to use this bond, to transform this familiar fetus with a series of overlays into the Fetal Detective.

Paul's main concern was with the willingness of the newcomers to participate in the promotion of the Fetal Detective. Paul had some unconventional ideas he had not yet revealed to anyone, and he wanted to be certain he had everyone on his side before he pursued them. Young Nicholas would not be a problem. He was amenable to most any suggestion, as long as it resulted in the furtherance of his creation. Paul could tell that the boy didn't have the blood of the lamb on him. It didn't matter. BOL owned the creation, and the creator. Any conversion would be a bonus.

He was less certain of Rance. The actor had been through the wars in his career, and apparently had split with Good Samaritan on a matter of principle. Very admirable, and hopefully whatever these principles were they would not prevent him from exploring the possibilities of the Fetal Detective to their fullest extent.

On the first day of shooting for *The Fetal Detective*, Rance found it easier to don the trench coat and fedora than to pull on the character of the womb-bound crusader. When he portrayed the Christus, he would prepare with prayer, Scripture-reading, and meditation. However, these devices were inappropriate for his new persona. He needed to develop an attitude, a dark angry fever.

Nick didn't make the situation any easier, constantly bursting into his dressing room to exclaim how he couldn't believe this was happening.

The fourth time it occurred, Rance said, "Look, kid, nothing is going to happen if you don't give me a few minutes by myself. I need to get into character. Maybe in the fifth sequel it will be second nature, but for now I need time to prepare."

"Sorry, sorry." The kid retreated.

Once the interruptions ceased, Rance thought of the logical technique to climb into his character. Something old, something new.

Rance closed his eyes and took some deep breaths, centering himself on the Unborn Avenger. The Fetal Detective is fear, the Fetal Detective is revenge, he thought. The Fetal Detective is within me. He contemplated mutilated innocent unborn babies for a second or two, then opened his eyes. Rance felt smaller, dangerous, and a great righteous rage filled him.

"It's payback time," Rance growled, and headed out to the set.

The shooting of *FD* proceeded rapidly, ahead of schedule. A happy marriage. To save on the expense of developing a mechanical fetus or hiring a midget to wear a fetus suit, Rance and a one hundred percent genuine innocent unborn aborted fetus were combined in a series of double-exposure shots. For those sequences which would be logistically impossible, such as the action scenes in the reproductive canal, Rance was filmed standing against a redbrick wall, relating the events in a whiskey-soaked monotone. This required superb storytelling skills, and Rance, the King of the Parable, was at his chilling, believable best.

Joshua Crippen proved to be a quality director, easily the equal of Elijah Winds. He knew what he wanted and didn't waste time getting it done. He was also amenable to the various suggestions Rance made on his character, and this was gold for any actor. It also made Rance more open to compromise. He had wanted the Pre-born Investigator to smoke a cigarette, like the private dicks of his youth, but Joshua convinced him that it would set a poor example for the children.

It was a wonderful time for Rance. BOL loved him, and it felt so good to be loved again, to be wanted, respected. It wasn't complicated. These were elemental needs that had to be fulfilled, they could not be denied. Rance fed on their love for a long time. He couldn't seem to get enough.

After the last day of shooting, the cast and crew got together and held the traditional funeral for the fetus. Rance and Nick tried to maintain a solemn disposition, but they had trouble keeping grins off their faces.

Afterward, they embraced. "You did it, kid, you did it," said Rance.

"It never would have happened without you," Nick replied, his voice pregnant with emotion. "You're the best."

"You're both pretty wonderful," Paul Pedphill said. He had come out of the BOL chapel and placed a hand on each of their shoulders. "I know if the little innocent unborn ones could talk, they would say, 'Thank you, Mr. Jericho and Mr. Puckett, for making a difference in my life.'"

Deciding who to invite to the first screening of *The Fetal Detective* was crucial. Paul had already previewed the film privately and was satisfied that it embodied the spirit of the original concept. It was always a struggle to look upon a finished work with fresh eyes. His initial exposure to the diminutive sleuth had been in written form, and so his own imagination had helped create the character. How would a virginal audience react?

BOL screenings were historically informal affairs, attended by BOL staff, a few critics, and a guest or two if any happened to be passing through town. For *The Fetal Detective*, though, Paul invited the leaders of preborn protection groups from all fifty states and, most importantly, the executive board of Christian Nation, the preeminent advocate of innocent unborn baby rights in the political sphere. The head of Christian Nation, Hyman Makover, spoke to millions of believers. If the Fetal Detective won the blessing of Hyman, his future would be golden indeed.

A week before the screening the tally showed that about thirty pro-innocent-unborn-baby leaders had accepted the invitation. It didn't hurt that BOL was providing complimentary airfare and lodging. No word had come yet from Christian Nation headquarters, and Paul had been stymied in his attempts to reach Hyman by conventional means, so he decided to be proactive in the matter.

First, he phoned Rance, explained the situation, and found him happy to make an unplanned personal appearance.

"I appreciate you checking with me first," said Rance. "At Good Samaritan they just issued marching orders without asking for my input."

"I'm surprised you tolerated them as long as you did," said Paul.

"Well, I became a pro at turning the other cheek."

"Those days are over, Rance."

"It will be strange for me. I've haven't done a personal appearance as anyone other than the Christus. I had the routine down. It was my whole identity for so many years. How should I act as the Fetal Detective? What should I do?"

"Hand out photos, sign autographs, say a few words on behalf of the five million innocent unborn babies that are murdered in this country every week. Think of it as just another job."

Rance said nothing.

"You know," said Paul, "the Fetal Detective has much in common with our Savior. The thirst for justice, the willingness to stand up for the rights of the innocent no matter what the odds. I'm sure you two will get along just fine."

Nicholas was even more of a pushover. His only concern was whether he could wear his official Fetal Detective T-shirt and baseball cap. The answer: Yes.

That only left the small matter of convincing Christian Nation how important it was that they view this film immediately.

"Mr. Makover has a very busy week, what with all the pending preborn legislation before Congress," said his secretary. "How about sometime next month?"

"Next month will be too late," Paul said. "I know we all have our jobs to do, and it's easy to get lost in our routines, but do you realize what's at stake here, ma'am? Just in the time we've been talking, a thousand innocent unborn babies have been slaughtered. Now I'm not saying it's your fault, but the sooner this movie is widely known, the sooner it has a chance to change hearts. And the sooner we change hearts, we're down to five hundred innocent unborn babies murdered in the time we've been talking. Do you want to be responsible for those five hundred extra lives that would have been saved if you hadn't refused my very generous offer? It's an eighty-minute movie. Isn't eighty minutes worth five hundred human lives?"

"Well, yes, but . . . "

"In fact, I was going to insist that we come out today, so we could save thousands more lives, but I realize people's schedules are tight."

"Yes, but . . . "

"Then we'll be there bright and early on Friday morning. If Mr. Makover doesn't like it, he can walk out, no hard feelings."

"What was the name of the movie again?"

"*The Fetal Detective.* Remember that name, you'll be hearing a lot of it in the weeks to come. It's the most important pro-life story ever put on film. Thank you for your time, ma'am. We'll see you first thing on Friday morning. Good-bye."

"But . . . "

Paul hung up the phone.

Yes, they would screen the film. Those five hundred babies spared the executioner's needle would see to that.

Thirty-Three

I FIGURED THE C IN C-SECTION STOOD FOR CHUMP. AND THE CHUMP WAS me. I don't know why I thought the docs would play by the rules. I'd seen them in action long enough to know better. But I thought even the docs would have limits. I was wrong.

I was waiting for them, hearing the tearing sounds as they started to slice their way through the abdomen, my best friend in one hand, a knuckle sandwich with extra mayhem in the other. Then everything got quiet. I stayed put. I could wait as long as they could. I wasn't going anywhere.

Suddenly a blinding light flashed from somewhere down below. I was disoriented for just a second, but that second was all it took. They got the drop on me. Strong, brutish hands grabbed my ankles and violently tugged me down. My gun went flying. I tried to grab hold of something, anything. I was falling.

They kept pulling until my head got stuck in the cervix, which they had so conveniently dilated. Good thing I was wearing my hat. It was dark again. I was cold.

I knew what was coming next. I couldn't believe it, but I knew.

Scissors would meet skull. They would puncture my soft cranium and suck out my brains so that my head would deflate like a dime store balloon. Then they would extract my corpse and dispose of it like any other preborn. Partial-birth abortion, they called it.

However, I wasn't too partial to that idea, so as I felt the cold steel ride up my spine, I twisted my body around and got my hands on the instrument of *death. The docs thought I was done for, but I had a few surprises left for them.*

I had to move fast, though. I thrust the scissors up until I hit flesh and bone. When I heard the scream, I cut my way free. As I did I felt a friendly nudge by my ear. Good friends have a way of helping you out when things get rough.

I was more than viable now. My preborn days were over. All the forces of dark medicine had been stacked against me. Dumpster city. Another fetus for the fire. Sorry to spoil your day, fellas.

Blam, blam, blam, blam.

It was a nice coming-out party.

The dame didn't like it, but then dames never do. I still depended on her, though, and not just because she had my hat.

I was in bad need of some R&R. I was tempted to tell the dame that we should blow this joint and find a beach in Acapulco where we could do the back-stroke in a pitcher of tequila. It would have been nice.

But this was no time to take it easy. Not with so many innocent lives on the line. Millions of my brothers and sisters weren't as lucky as me. Millions more were facing death every week.

There was work to be done.

The lights came up in a meeting room at the headquarters of Christian Nation in Washington, D.C. The executive board huddled briefly, heads close and nodding, then one by one they filed out of the room, expressionless, until the only persons remaining were Hyman Makover, Rance Jericho, Nick Puckett, and Paul Pedphill. Paul was puzzled by their response. They hadn't reacted at all during the screening. For some reason BOL feature films tended to polarize viewers. A noncommittal response was rare. He looked over at Rance and Nick and shrugged.

Then Hyman Makover approached Paul. He was an impressive man, dressed in a white shirt and dark tie, his lips thin and wet. He looked at the president of Blood of the Lamb Pictures with an odd smile and said quietly, "Of course, you realize that we can't take an official position on this film."

"You can't?"

"No, we can't."

"Didn't you like it?"

"It was very . . . interesting." He stuck out his pale hand. "I appreciate you folks coming all the way out here to show it to us."

Paul shook the hand without enthusiasm. "You're welcome, but I was hoping you might be able to help us out from a publicity standpoint. You have such a large mailing list."

"Yes, we do."

"We agree that the nation is at a crossroads, don't we?"

"Yes, it is."

"And that the slaughter of innocent unborn babies is the most important issue of our time?"

Hyman winced. "Please."

"What's wrong?"

"That's such a provocative way of phrasing the problem."

"Provocative?"

"We prefer a gentler, less confrontational approach," said Hyman. "*Slaughter* is so harsh. We like to say the baby has been *unmade*."

Paul frowned in a major way.

"Don't be fooled by our use of the language," said Hyman. "We're as dedicated to the cause of the unborn as you are. It's why we're here, our whole reason for being."

"It sounds like a full-scale retreat to me."

"This isn't middle America, Mr. Pedphill. We can accomplish more by not going out of our way to offend people. We try to avoid the A-word altogether, actually. It's so much easier to gain a sympathetic hearing when you put a softer tinge on the gruesome realities."

"Then the Fetal Detective isn't going to get your cooperation?"

"Let's just say your detective walks meaner streets than we like."

So Paul Pedphill had to regroup. On the flight back home, he decided that if the high rollers in the anti-innocent-unborn-baby-murdering movement weren't going to help, he would take the Fetal Detective to the grunts on the front lines of this holy war, to the very places where those babies were unmade.

Revenge of the Unborn

Thirty-Four

IN SPITE OF HIS PRAYERS AND BEST INTENTIONS, LEVITICUS WAS UNABLE to rid his life of the Fetal Detective. For Leviticus possessed a mailbox and cable television and open eyes. He had attempted to secure himself in the good community of believers, the gentle lambs, thinking he could keep the angry lambs at bay. But the Fetal Detective would not be denied.

The Fetal Detective was the focus of the largest and most astonishing publicity campaign Leviticus had ever witnessed. Flyer after flyer showed up in the Specks' mailboxes at work and home, counting down the days to the arrival of the Unborn Avenger, as they were calling him now. He made several appearances on the cover of *Christian Film Review,* and inside there were long, worshipful articles on "the most innovative Christian film in years," complete with color-photo spreads and interviews with the creators and cast and just coincidentally ads for FETAL DETECTIVE™ bumper stickers and buttons and baseball caps.

The Not-Quite-Born-One also made appearances in publications including *Christian Women Today, Pulpit and Pew,* and, most sadly, *Christian Bus Driver.* "Former *CBD* Staffer Making Movie History." Leviticus couldn't blame Bob Countenance for feeling a sense of pride.

And the billboards. They seemed to be undergoing transformations on a daily basis.

Rocked by this promotional assault, Leviticus would lie on his bed late into the night, wondering if he could have done anything to stop the Fetal Detective, wondering why he wanted to so intensely. Would Blood of the Lamb, through the charms of this preborn pest, change the tenor of inspirational films and drive Good Samaritan out of business? Possibly, although Leviticus usually kept the business end of Good Samaritan on a more analytical level. He was more worried about the impact of a disaffected Rick Bible abandoning his career as a Christus.

Was it the fact that Rance and Nick defected to BOL, had literally run out on him? No, he had made his peace with that. It had been wrong to deceive the young writer. His opinion of Rance certainly had not changed. He had a right to make a living. If Dad hadn't been so narrow-minded about Rance's talent, had shown even a modest interest in keeping his biggest star happy, Rance might not have been forced to look beyond the loving arms of Good Samaritan for comfort.

What about the frustration that Good Samaritan wasn't able to make the film? Maybe. Leviticus appreciated the story on a certain intellectual level, although he wasn't sure where that level might be. Some other world, perhaps.

Or maybe it was the abortion issue itself. He didn't think so, though. Not being a woman, Leviticus found it difficult to visualize the reproductive process. He had never witnessed an abortion, never knew anyone who had had one. From everything he had read and heard, it wasn't a pleasant process, certainly nothing to celebrate. But the leap from that modest sentiment to the spirit of the Fetal Detective was unimaginably great.

Leviticus didn't really think the Fetal Detective advocated the killing of physicians. Fetuses do not carry guns, yet the fetus did all the shooting. A dichotomy. The work was a power fantasy, not a call for social action. The Fetal Detective was an antihero in a long tradition of antiheroes. Like Robin Hood. Until now, Christianity

didn't share in that tradition (well, maybe Judas, in a certain per-
verse way). It was what made the Fetal Detective, and the mind of
Nicholas Puckett, potentially so dangerous. What creation would
Nick unleash on the world next? Maybe the Fetal Detective would
be the beginning and the end; if so, that was enough.

But how could anyone not see the irony? Even the most ardent
right-to-lifers didn't believe a fetus was capable of that much independence. Who knows, the Fetal Detective might even turn out to
be a force for good, an outlet for the most angry lambs. They could
live out their most visceral, violent fantasies through him.

Yet none of these options felt like it held the true answer. What
other factor was he missing? Leviticus didn't know.

What capped off this blizzard of publicity was the day Leviticus received the flyer in the mail promoting the Fetal Detective's
upcoming personal appearance outside the Hilltop Health Clinic,
located not five miles from the Good Samaritan studios. Talk about
nerve. The event was planned in conjunction with a round of
protests at the clinic. There was a whole list of dates at health cen-
ters throughout the Midwest. Free autographed photos of the Unborn Avenger. Hot dogs. Balloons for the kids.

Was Rance going to be there, in character? Leviticus badly
wanted to see Rance, talk to him, but not like that.

Leviticus tossed the flyer into the trash, along with the rest of
them, like so many murdered babies. He didn't reserve the date on
his calendar, and when the day came he didn't even watch the
news. He tried to ignore the whole thing. It was a fad, nothing
more.

Good Samaritan would outlive any fad. The initial orders for
Eyesore for God had been slow, but any day now they would come
flooding in. *Eyesore* was the first inspirational film with a strong en-
vironmental theme. Now *that* was innovation.

Thirty-Five

THE UNBORN AVENGER TOUR KICKED OFF IN FRIENDLY TERRITORY, Blood of the Lamb's hometown of Nashville. Paul Pedphill picked up Rance at his apartment and drove him to the site. Rance was in full costume. He looked nervous.

"These are uncharted waters for all of us, Rance. Maybe it won't work out, and we'll have to try something else. But remember, these are our people, and you will be their hero. Perhaps all we'll hear today are the silent screams of the preborn. Soon, though, the screams will be ones of delight."

"I'm sure it will be fine," said Rance, adjusting his fedora in the visor mirror. "You can't imagine what a relief it is, playing a role like this. I got so tired of people wanting me to bless them every time I turned around."

When they arrived at the clinic on King Street, next door to the Jolly Troll Smorgasbord, there were a dozen or so protesters marching on the sidewalk across the street. They bore signs expressing such sentiments as ABORTION IS MURDER; ADOPT, DON'T AS-SASSINATE; and REMEMBER THE BABY.

"We're going to have to copyright that slogan one of these days," said Paul, parking at a nearby supermarket lot.

They left the car and walked over to the protesters, Paul toting a bagful of freebies, the looks of the righteous ones growing odder as the pair from BOL approached.

"Hey, folks, has anyone here heard of *The Fetal Detective?*" asked Paul. A couple of confirming nods, as they kept marching. "Well, it's only the most important preborn film ever released. The Fetal Detective is the first hero of the pro-life movement. He's sworn to fight for the rights of the unborn, and he's got a sense of humor, too. This gentleman here is Rance Jericho, Christian film legend, who stars in the movie. Do you have anything to say to these people, Rance?"

"It's payback time," the former Christus growled.

"I've got a ton of giveaways for you dedicated souls today," said Paul. "Autographed photos, pens, key chains, bumper stickers . . . "

That last item was too tempting. The marchers broke off from their vigil and gathered around Paul and Rance. "No need to crowd, folks, plenty to go around. Got a camera? Take a picture with the man who plays the Fetal Detective, without doubt the most amazing pro-innocent-unborn-baby story ever filmed. It's coming out this week, and you don't have to go to your local church to see it, because it's available right now on home video, and there's even a five-dollar discount coupon on your flyer. Just cut it out and send it in. Don't you dare miss it. Buy it for your whole family, but see it for the little ones."

When the bag was empty, and the marchers resumed their posts, Paul and Rance headed back to the car. "That wasn't too bad, was it?" asked Paul. "You looked like you were enjoying yourself."

"The attention was nice," said Rance. "I missed it. It's been so long."

"It's only going to get bigger," Paul said.

Following this successful promotion, Paul assigned a subordinate to accompany Rance to abortion protests across the state. Reports back were positive, so Paul sent Rance on a nationwide tour, putting an emphasis on the South and the Midwest.

In the meantime, orders for the inaugural adventure of the Unborn Avenger were coming in strong. Already it appeared as if sales would easily outstrip BOL's previous best-seller, *Die, Baby, Die!*

The groundwork thus laid with the true believers, Paul Pedphill decided it was time to introduce the Unborn Avenger to the sinful, secular world. Soon, every kid in America would be driving his or her parents crazy with the slogan, "It's payback time."

Thirty-Six

Janey goin' down to the abortion clinic
Gonna kill her baby
She don't want to be no mother
Gonna kill her baby
It's a child not a choice
Let's all sing it with one clear voice
Janey goin' down to the abortion clinic
Gonna see the baby-killin' man. . . .
—Traditional pro-life spiritual (Anonymous)

"I REALLY THINK WE SHOULD WAIT," SAID EVIE, HESITATING OUTSIDE
the door.

"We can't wait," Rick Bible said, patting her stomach through
her parka. "You're already starting to show. He's going to figure it
out sooner or later."

"I don't know. I'm scared. He's going to be mad."

"I'll handle everything," said Rick, opening the door to the
Speck house and leading her inside. "Don't you worry about a
thing."

"I mean," she said, dropping her voice to a whisper, "he hasn't
even figured out that we're dating. Maybe we should just tell him
that today, and wait with the rest until later. A lot later."

"Why not get it all taken care of today?"

"Is that you, Evie?" came a voice from the kitchen.

"Yes, Dad, it's me. Rick's here, too."

"Wonderful," said Noah. "Come on in. I just made a fresh pot of coffee. I'm rewriting the ending of *Picture Window of God*."

"We'll be right there," Evie called out, drawing Rick away from the kitchen and taking him up the dark stairs.

"What are you doing?" asked Rick.

At the first landing, she took his hands in her own and said, "I don't think this is the right time to tell him." Rick's beatific face was washed in moonlight; she had to turn away.

"Why wait?"

"Because I'm . . . " Now she looked at him squarely. "I'm not sure I want to have a baby right now."

She felt him stiffen. His hands seemed colder. "I haven't made a decision, I just don't know. We didn't plan this. I wasn't expecting it."

"I didn't know you were thinking about . . . ending it."

"Well, we haven't been doing so well lately," Evie said slowly. "You know that. Maybe things will seem clearer once we get our own situation resolved. I don't want to hurry that part, but I really need to take action *here*." She stroked her mildly protruding abdomen. "I'm not going to be getting any smaller."

He looked at her with hurt eyes. "Does this mean you've changed the way you feel about me?"

"We're changing as people," she said. "I want to hang onto what we had as much as you do. But our lives are changing. You're not the same person as when I first met you. Neither am I." She blinked away tears. "I made an appointment for tomorrow with someone who can advise me about my pregnancy. The risks, the mental part, the future. I'm so confused sometimes. I don't even know how to think about it. They'll be able to help."

"I'm going down to the clinic this morning," Evie told the other founding member of her two-person Women of Christus, Et Al. support group.

"How did your beau take it?"

"Not really well," said Evie. "He thinks my indecision has something to do with the problems we've been having. Which is probably true."

"Does he care if you have the baby?"

"I'm not sure. I don't know that he's thinking about it any more clearly than I am."

"Well, I just want you to know, Evie, that the West Coast Islam branch of the Women of Christus is behind you."

"Thanks. It's nice to have an official support group at a time like this."

Evie drove to the clinic, clutching a yellow piece of paper with the name of the counselor she was supposed to meet, a Monica Audubon, and a list of questions. The inquiries ranged from the medical to the spiritual. Evie figured her counselor wouldn't have answers for all of them, but it wouldn't hurt to ask.

After parking in the small lot on the side of the low, nondescript building, Evie walked around to the front entrance. She signed in at the desk and a few minutes later a tall, freckled woman, her red hair tied back in a ponytail, came into the waiting area. She was wearing a kelly green skiing sweater and a white turtleneck.

"Hi, are you Evie?"

"Yes, that's me."

They shook hands.

"I'm Monica. Come on back."

Evie followed the woman down the hall to a cramped office. A poster on the wall for National Birth Control Month showed a pregnant nursery-rhyme character and the poem:

> *There was an old woman who lived in a shoe.*
> *She had so many children she didn't know what to do.*
> *Hadn't she ever heard of a condom?*

"So, Evie," said Monica, as they sat down, "what can I do for you today?"

Evie looked away, embarrassed.

"How many months pregnant are you?"

Glancing down at herself, Evie said, "Three, I think. It's getting pretty obvious, I guess."

"Are you seeing a doctor?"

"Well, not really. I mean I did, but I haven't gone back."

"I'd highly recommend it. I can give you a referral if you don't have a regular physician."

"Thank you." Unfolding her piece of paper, Evie said, "I have some questions."

"Okay. Understand, Evie, that anything you say here won't leave this room. So feel free to talk to me."

Evie squinted at the paper. Her notes had been handwritten, and the sweat from her hand caused the ink to smear. Refolding the paper, she said, "I guess, I guess I just need someone to talk to, someone who has . . . facts. I don't want to sound foolish, but I'm having a hard time making a decision about the pregnancy. I want to know what my options are, what the risks are."

"It's a big decision, an important commitment. Have you had a child before?"

"No?"

"Are you in a long-term relationship?"

Evie hesitated, then said, "I'm not sure. Sometimes I think I am. Lately . . . I, I just don't know." She swallowed hard. "My boyfriend's line of work is creating some conflict between us."

"What does he do for a living?"

"He portrays our Lord and Savior, Jesus Christ." When she saw the befuddled look on Monica's face, Evie elaborated. "He's a film actor. We both work for an inspirational film company."

The counselor smiled. "I certainly can see the potential for conflict there."

"It is complicating things," said Evie.

"My second cousin's first husband used to do a one-man show as Abraham Lincoln at an amusement park."

"You're kidding!" Evie sat forward. "Then you know how I feel. You know exactly how I feel."

"Well, I heard a couple of stories."

"Listen, I run a support group for the women of men who portray Christ, only there's just two of us and the other person's partner doesn't portray Jesus at all, but Muhammad, and I've been thinking maybe I should let more people in, not be so strict about membership requirements, maybe include anyone who's involved with an actor who plays the same legendary figure on a continuous basis, I mean, they all have their unique problems, like mine is the Son of God and he doesn't always leave his sandals and robe at the office, if you know what I mean, and the guy who played Lincoln would probably be spouting bromides in the bedroom all the time, only where would you draw the line, I mean, I can see Abraham Lincoln, he's up there certainly, but how about someone like Harry Truman, or even Samuel Clemens, famous men, no doubt about it, but they'd probably be more annoying at home than a source of spiritual turmoil."

"Yes, that's probably true."

"So do you want to be a member of our group? I know you're just related to someone whose partner portrayed Abraham Lincoln, but you could be a supporting member. It doesn't cost any-

thing to join. I suppose all this sounds really selfish and everything, like I'm the one with the cross to bear."

"It's good that you're in a support group," Monica said. "Sometimes just one person can make a huge difference in your life."

Thirty minutes later, her purse bulging with informational
brochures, Evie left the clinic. She walked around the building to
the parking lot, feeling more at peace than she had in weeks. The
counselor offered no answer to the ultimate question, though. Evie
wasn't disappointed. She knew she'd have to make that decision by
herself. What she did leave with was the counselor's experience
with hundreds of other women and a sense that she wasn't the only
one ever in this situation. It was a good feeling.

As Evie headed across the lot to her car, she noticed a man with
white hair, gold-rimmed glasses, and a blue parka walking toward
her. As they were about to cross paths, their eyes met. He smiled
at her, and she smiled in return.

Then, out of the corner of her eye, she saw a flash of movement, from the edge of the lot. Before she could turn, a rapid series of pops sounded and something with razor teeth bit into her
torso and her legs. She heard cries, from her own throat or someone else's she didn't know. She had a vague sense of falling, and as
the pain drifted away, her body filled up with a great darkness, and
then, strangely, a source of light.

Thirty-Seven

From the pages of the *Preborn Times*, the weekly newspaper of the anti-innocent-unborn-baby-murdering movement:

It may have been a case of friendly fire.

One innocent unborn baby, name and gender undetermined, was killed when gunfire accidentally broke out in the parking lot of an abortion mill in Coon Rapids, Minnesota, last Monday.

The incident began when a helpless baby was being hauled into the mill by an abortionist and an unidentified woman. What happened next is unclear. Sources who asked that their names not be used told PT that a well-meaning individual apparently tried to save the baby when a gun discharged. It is not known if the gun belonged to the abortionist or the Good Samaritan.

"We can take comfort knowing that the innocent baby died in a far more humane way than if he or she would have made it into the mill and been subjected to the tortures of the abortionist," said Frank Zachariah, head of the Minnesota Innocent Unborn Babies' Rights League. "God must have been watching over the little one." Zachariah added that a memorial service for the baby would be held next Thursday at the MIUBRL headquarters in Mound.

Thirty-Eight

"IT WAS SO STRANGE, SO STRANGE," EVIE KEPT SAYING WEAKLY.

"Don't try to talk, hon, just rest," Rick Bible said, sitting at her bedside in the hospital, holding her thin hand. He hadn't let go of it since she left surgery.

"Why didn't she tell me?" whispered Noah, his face ashen and drawn, as he stood with Leviticus by the dark window. "I would have understood."

"She was afraid," said Leviticus. "She didn't want you to think she was being selfish."

"This is my fault. If she would have felt comfortable enough to talk to me, this never would have happened."

"Don't blame yourself, Dad. You didn't know."

"So strange."

The bullets did considerable damage to Evie. She had been struck in the abdomen, resulting in a violent miscarriage. Another bullet tore into her upper thigh, causing a loss of blood but no major trauma. Unfortunately, one of the bullets found its way to her lower spinal cord. She could still move from the waist up. Her legs were useless. The doctor said the paralysis was permanent.

The other victim, a Dr. Jonathan Bovary, died instantly. The gunman escaped. Nobody saw him, they only heard the shots.

"I felt myself falling," said Evie. "Not in slow motion, very fast. I don't remember hitting the ground. Everything got dark. I was floating, in the darkness. Then I saw the light. Narrow at first, like a flashlight. I began walking toward it. The light got bigger and bigger, and I followed it, as if I were going down a long tunnel. There was a person in the light, but it was so bright all I could see was a silhouette."

"Who was it, Evie?" Rick asked.

"I'm not sure," she said. "I came back to my body before I could see who it was. All I could tell was that the person was very small, almost like a child, and he was wearing a hat."

Leviticus knew the identity of the entity at the end of the tunnel, and it became clear to him at last where the journey of the last year was leading him. There was a menace on the loose, a preborn terror turning good people upside down and corrupting everything it touched.

Through constant exposure to the barrage of mutilated fetuses and hate hidden in love's swaddling clothes, the Christian community had become numbed to the warped sensibilities of the fetus-first congregation. What was once shocking was now mundane. And the next step had been taken, as embodied in the spirit of the Unborn Avenger. Soon, he too, would become a part of the tattered fabric of everyday life in America.

But not if Leviticus Speck could help it. God had finally answered his prayers. Leviticus wasn't sure if he believed that every tragedy was God's will, he had never thought so. However, he wondered if God had given the Speck family this horrible gift in order to ensure that the diminutive sleuth would not go unchallenged. Am I that weak? Leviticus wondered. If saving Good Samaritan wasn't enough of a reason to take action, he had plenty of reasons now. He was feeling some righteous anger himself.

Because Leviticus knew who crippled Evie and killed the doctor.

This was no longer an intellectual struggle or a battle for moral truth.

This was *personal*.

Thirty-Nine

IT HAD BEEN A LONG WINTER, QUIET DAYS PUNCTUATED WITH moments of pure dread, like the thunderous cracking of ice when you walk across a lake in January. Leviticus had been on his first case less than a week. A washed-up Christus portraying a fetus with a severe psychological problem. He was heading up a gang of thugs that was causing trouble from the redwood forests to the Blue Ridge Family Planning Clinic. He may have been a toddler, but there was nothing cute about him.

It wasn't hard to track the kid down; he wasn't exactly trying to keep a low profile. He was bold, maybe a little too bold. He was leaving a trail, and Leviticus picked up on it right away. Their operation seemed to run like this: The boss comes into a town and fires up the locals, then makes a quick exit before the trouble begins. And there is trouble. Shootings, assaults, bombings, general mayhem. But he keeps his hands clean, lets his underlings do the dirty work.

Leviticus haunted antiabortion rallies and meetings, showing an old photo of the Christus to everyone he came across. Look familiar? He usually didn't, but there was enough hesitation, enough sideways glances, to reassure Leviticus that he was on the right path.

From Rapid City to Des Moines to Topeka, Leviticus followed

the bloody trail. He knew he was closing in. There was an energy among the faithful, a sense of renewed motivation.

Then, in Tulsa, the trail ended.

It was a cool, windy afternoon, and Leviticus was feeling the effects of too many two-lane highways and cheap motels. The clinic was set on the borderline between a shady residential area and a strip of fast-food joints and video stores. There was a line across the street from the clinic, and they weren't waiting to get in.

As he cruised by, looking for a place to park, Leviticus thought he spotted a figure in a trenchcoat and hat among the protesters. Quickly, he pulled over to the curb and walked back up the street. He brought along a good friend. It's always wise to have a traveling companion.

Leviticus hurried over to the crowd, clutching his friend, black and heavy, in his hand. The protesters were chanting, "Two, four, six, eight, do not vacuum aspirate!" On one of their signs a bloody child's doll was affixed, arms akimbo, eyes plucked from their sockets. Leviticus wound his way through their ranks until he came up behind the man in the trenchcoat. He grabbed the man's arm.

"Rance . . . "

The Fetal Detective turned.

It wasn't Rance.

This Unborn Avenger was younger than Rance, taller, and had a weaker chin and much thinner lips.

The Fetal Detective regarded Leviticus without alarm, as if he was practiced at such intrusions. He reached into the pocket of his trenchcoat.

"It's payback time," growled the Unborn Avenger, and handed Leviticus an autographed photo.

When he got back to his car, Leviticus thumbed through the Bible he had planned to give to Rance until he found the Book of Job. He sat in the car and read until it grew dark and his own troubles seemed less unsurmountable.

Forty

WILL PLAY GOD FOR FOOD

The line at the drive-thru was long, but it wasn't so bad without a car. Once, his future stretched before him like the road to Nashville, and everything seemed possible in his improbable life. Now, now . . .

A horn blared.

"Move it, you idiot!"

Jerry Fudd wound through the line of automobiles idling under the big sun, the asphalt burning his bare feet, getting closer, closer to the ordering board.

Once, his fedora was poised cockily on his shorn head, and his gun was polished and fully loaded, if only with blanks.

Reaching the board, Jerry squinted at the menu. He could barely make out the oversized photos of burgers and nuggets and drinks, and the captions were indecipherable. The honking became more insistent.

"Welcome to Fat Boy, can I take your order?"

Order. Was there an order to things? Or was it all disorder?

"Hello? Can I take your order, please?"

Take my order.

"No! You can't have it!" Jerry screamed into the speaker and got out of there in a hurry.

WILL PLAY GOD FOR GOOD FOOD
WILL PLAY THE FOOL FOR GOD
WILL PLAY THE FOOL FOR GOLD
WILL PLAY GOD FOR GOLD
WILL PLAY GOD FOR GOOD
And other poems by Jerry Fudd

Jerry Fudd feared the supermarket, among other places and people and thoughts and feelings. Piggly Wigglys were the worst. Those goddamn Piggly Wigglys.

Even though he was famished, Jerry couldn't bring himself to pass through the swine's automatic doors. He found a nice shady spot between a newspaper dispenser and a soda machine and waited until the fear became tamed.

He entertained thoughts of beer. Beer in glasses, bottles, cans. Beer by the case, by the keg, by the brewery. Dark beer, light beer, beer that you couldn't see at all.

A good spot to sit, to watch. People would enter empty-handed and depart with more than they could carry. It was strange, so much like his own life. But he feared Piggly Wiggly because he didn't know what they wanted to steal from him. He didn't know if he had anything left for them to take.

People mostly ignored him. He wasn't begging for food or money, he was just sitting there. The pop machine—well, that certainly made some interesting noises. Once a man tossed a quarter at Jerry, and he watched with disinterest as it struck the clear door of the newspaper dispenser and flipped into a mound of mulch below the curb.

One sweltering day Jerry was nestled in his usual niche, tracking a seagull as it pecked at fast-food wrappers, when he spotted a woman across the shimmering parking lot. She was staring at him.

The woman was thin and pale, wearing an untucked white shirt and sunglasses . . . and staring at him.

Nothing new about that—Jerry had been on the receiving end of some mighty odd looks since he had taken up his position, and always when he met their gaze, the prying eyes would dart away. But not this woman. If anything, her body language grew even more focused on him.

After this first encounter, and the others that followed, a car or truck would intervene, blocking his view of her. By the time the shopper entered empty-handed and returned with more than he or she could carry, the woman would be gone.

Jerry began to wonder if he was hallucinating. A person goes without beer long enough and who knows what effect it has on the brain.

Then one day the strange woman approached him.

"Are you waiting for someone?" she asked, smiling.

Suddenly it occurred to him that she was a Piggly Wiggly spy. A plainclothes security guard sent to evict him from his spot, drive him out.

He crossed his arms. "Nope. I'm just sitting here. No law against sitting, not hurting you, no sir."

"I wouldn't hurt you, either."

As she stepped onto his curb, sunlight glinted off a silver crucifix dangling from a dull chain around her neck. It swayed, and he stared at it until she left.

The next day, or so it seemed, the woman returned, saying, "How are you doing today, Jerry?"

He regarded her strangely. He didn't think he had revealed his name to her. In fact, he was pretty sure of it. He didn't remember telling her. He might have. He didn't know. These days were so hard to distinguish. How long had he been manning his Piggly Wiggly post? And how many times had he seen this mysterious woman, this mirage?

"I'm hungry," he said without self-pity.

So she brought him food.

The next day it was raining and chilly; she gave him the yellow poncho she was wearing, and trotted away bare-armed through the downpour.

"I'm not a good person," he told her on a nicer day.

She smiled.

"I've done wrong. People have gotten hurt because of things I've done, people I've cared about."

"Try this bread," she said, tearing off a hunk from the loaf she was toting and passing it to him.

"Isn't it good?"

He chewed slowly, nodding.

"I've noticed your jewelry," he told her later. "You're going to try to convert me, aren't you? Who are you working for? What are you selling? Give me your tracts and leave me alone."

"I don't have much to give you," she said apologetically, the smile fading. "I give you what I can."

Jerry kept waiting for the pitch, but it never came.

"Who sent you here?"

The woman shrugged. "I saw you." She slipped off her sunglasses, and for the first time Jerry met her eyes. They were brown and full, and both warmed his heart and made him sad.

"I'm not some bum who needs a handout," he told her. "Do you know who I am? Who do you think I am? What do you think I want? Why are you here?"

"I saw you," she said again.

On his last day with the strange woman, the day Jerry finally passed through the automatic doors of Piggly Wiggly and filled his cart, she bowed her head and removed the chain, carefully placing it around his neck.

He held the sign between his fingers. "Will I see you again?"

"Of course. I love you." In her eyes was neither lust nor marriage nor paternal instinct.

Jerry didn't understand her, in spite of his résumé.

She touched his hand, then drifted away across the bright expanse of the Piggly Wiggly parking lot. Jerry watched her until she crossed the street and disappeared in a maze of cars outside a doughnut shop and dry-cleaning store.

Is it that simple? he wondered, clutching the symbol on the chain. It can't be that simple. What about movies and mailing lists and cable networks and books? What about nice homes and cars and clothes and obedience? And what about beer?

"I saw you," she had said.

I saw you.

Forty-One

It was a time of healing for the Speck family. Evie returned home from the hospital in fair spirits, although her prognosis had not changed. She told everyone she felt lucky to be alive. Behind her eyes, Leviticus thought, dwelt a profound sadness. Rick had moved into a spare upstairs bedroom so that he could tend to her. Her absence meant a larger workload for the rest of them. Leviticus didn't mind; this was a good time to be lost in one's work.

Good Samaritan would muddle along. The market for innocent inspirational films had abruptly shrunk with the new wave of graphic, in-your-face exploitation films which the Fetal Detective was spawning, but there would always be a place for Good Samaritan, if only to fill up a slot on a youth-night schedule, if only ordered for amusement. Leviticus had accepted the fact that Good Samaritan would no longer be a major force in Christian cinema. The world had changed too much, and it showed no signs of wanting to return to its gentler past. The most Good Samaritan could hope for was to be the still small voice in the back of the minds of the angry lambs. It gave Leviticus some comfort to think this was true.

At the conclusion of one of these long, inward-looking days, Leviticus returned to the farmhouse well after midnight. There were still

lights on, in the kitchen and upstairs. Leviticus went inside. His father was sitting at the kitchen table, going over the books.

"Hey, Dad."

"Go to bed, Leviticus."

"I had a few things to finish up on the promotion for *Picture
Window of God.* Evie gave me all sorts of ideas. I think she's getting
pretty impatient about getting back to work."

"That's good news. She must be feeling better."

Leviticus yawned. "I'm going to call it a night. You should go
to bed, too."

"I won't be long. Good night, son."

" 'Night."

Leviticus headed upstairs. As he went down the hallway to his
room, he passed by Evie's door, which was ajar. He hesitated. She
was propped up in bed, her long white nightshirt rolled up high on
her thighs. Kneeling at her bedside, Rick stroked her thin pale legs
with both hands. He was wearing his robe and sandals.

"Can you feel that?" he quietly asked her. "Can you feel anything?"

"It's okay," she said. "I'm getting used to being this way. I
really am."

"If I hadn't doubted my role as the Christus, if I had just accepted the gift that had been given to me, then maybe God would
have given me the power to help you."

"Don't, Rick. Please."

"I want to be the Christus. It's what I was meant to be. I see that
now. I don't care if I ever get another part the rest of my life." He
returned his attention to her legs. "Can you feel this? Can you feel
anything at all?"

Leviticus retreated from the doorway and went to his room. He
tried to sleep, but he felt too disturbed inside. He wanted to pray,
to ask the Lord to give Rick and Evie comfort, but he couldn't concentrate. He needed to walk and think. He left his room.

The lights were off in the rest of the house. Leviticus quietly stepped downstairs and went outside through the kitchen into the cool spring night. He could hear the steady rush of highway traffic in the distance. The yard was muddy. Leviticus walked along gingerly, hands in his pockets.

He walked until the house was no longer in sight, cutting through a boggy ditch to the highway. He wanted to walk forever down a dark road. There was no peace in his heart, and he couldn't live without peace in his heart. The pain in the world wracked his soul. It wasn't just spiritual or emotional, it was actual physical pain. His chest felt tight, constricted. His faith would always ride to the rescue in times like these, but now he didn't feel it. He was thoughtful, shot with conscience, not willing to be soothed with that familiar grace, the peace that passes all understanding.

He walked.

Head down, headlights from the oncoming traffic flashing across his feet, Leviticus didn't spot the billboard until he was almost upon it.

When he did see it, he simply walked on, passing by the scaffolding, going from the dark side to the light. Preoccupied, he didn't think about it again until he suddenly got the feeling he was being watched.

Leviticus stopped.

He turned.

Leviticus found himself face-to-face with the source of his pain, although the kid's face was the size of a truck, bathed in a series of spotlights. He was looking down upon his former nemesis with great pleased eyes, godlike and triumphant.

But this billboard had changed. Again.

AMERICA'S FAVORITE FETUS IS BACK!
THE FETAL DETECTIVE II: REVENGE OF THE UNBORN

Leviticus stared at the billboard for a long time, hoping for a vision, praying it would transform into something loving and benign. He shut his eyes.

A carload of yelling teenagers sped by. One of them shouted something at Leviticus, then a plastic pop bottle skipped across the shoulder of the road, tumbling to a rest at his feet. He glanced back at the car as it disappeared around a curve, then bent down and retrieved the bottle. Didn't they know it was wrong to litter? Without looking up he turned and passed over to the dark side of the billboard, clutching the dirty pop bottle to his aching chest, heading for home.

ABOUT THE AUTHOR

David Prill grew up in Bloomington, Minnesota, and attended a variety of colleges before graduating from the University of Minnesota with a degree in journalism. The political humor column he wrote for the *Minnesota Daily* earned him a Best Columnist award from the Minnesota Newspaper Association in 1991. He also spent a year working on a weekly newspaper in St. James, Minnesota, before he turned to writing fiction; during this time he covered such events as the Watonwan County Fair, Railroad Days, and the Lost City.

David Prill's first novel, *The Unnatural,* won a Minnesota Book Award and was called "The funniest novel about the funeral business since *The Loved One*" by *The New York Times.* His second novel, *Serial Killer Days,* was published to similar acclaim.